Wish you were here

COME WITH GETAWAY TOURS FOR EXCITING ADVENTURES IN THE MOST EXOTIC PLACES— IT'S THE ULTIMATE WAY TO SEE THE WORLD!

MEET THE GANG:

LUCI always thought her life was so **normal**. She can't wait to travel, meet new people and experience different cultures— the tour is her dream come true!

JAY's mother is white and her father is black. Being different has made her strong and independent; she's the voice of reason to all the kids on the tour.

STACEY is the epitome of California glamour. Whether sitting in a bistro or touring a medieval castle, she's beautifully dressed, perfectly made-up—and ready to flirt.

DARIA thinks her wealthy rancher father sent her on the tour to punish her. She finds a friend in Stacey, who also has a powerful—and sometimes distant—father.

AIMEE's post–New Wave style and permanent headphones may give the impression that she's tuning out, but she's actually very smart and very tuned **in**.

GLIN is a long-haired guy from Vermont. Though his medieval wardrobe makes him stand out from the crowd, Luci thinks he's gorgeous **and** fascinating.

LOGAN is a man's man. He camps, climbs, flies, boats, and everything in between. His idea of love is a natural girl, so why is **Stacey** hitting on him?

TIM and **FRANCINE ATKINSON** are the young, married, Getaway tour guides. They're fun, adventurous, and best of all, they avoid tourist traps like the plague!

Don't miss

W

Wish NS

Wish you were here:

FRANCE

ROBIN O'NEILL

B

BERKLEY BOOKS, NEW YORK

WISH YOU WERE HERE: FRANCE

A Berkley Book / published by arrangement with
the author

PRINTING HISTORY
Berkley edition / July 1996

The Putnam Berkley World Wide Web site address is
http://www.berkley.com

ISBN: 0-425-14944-7

BERKLEY®
Berkley Books are published by The Berkley Publishing Group,
200 Madison Avenue, New York, New York 10016.
BERKLEY and the "B" design
are trademarks belonging to Berkley Publishing Corporation.

PRINTED IN THE UNITED STATES OF AMERICA

10 9 8 7 6 5 4 3 2

To Dr. Hugh Riordan, Dr. Ron Hunninghake and
The Center for the Improvement of Human Functioning

ACKNOWLEDGMENTS

I would like to thank Alma Ohnemiller and Mary and Larry Aue for opening their hearts and homes to us this year. It was an act of generosity beyond measure.

I would also like to thank all the wonderful people at Berkley who helped every step along the way: Laura Anne Gilman, Maria Vlasak, the people in the design department and those in the sales department. It's great to be part of such a fine team.

Jack Remick and Guy Melancon.

Jim Alexander.

Cyberbuddy Jeffd.

Ivy and Fifi.

Robin and Sasha and Happy.

And, of course, Randy, and Fortune Pawlowski.

Chapter One

"**I**'ll never make this flight!"

Sixteen-year-old Luci McKennitt could barely sit still. She opened her flight bag at least fifteen times, and checked her purse so many times to touch her passport and airline ticket that her mother finally put her hand over Luci's.

It was dusk as they began to circle through John F. Kennedy International Airport. The traffic swirled into a kaleidoscope of color, with yellow taxis zipping between buses and airport shuttles.

Mrs. McKennitt smiled. "You *will* make the flight."

Luci glanced at her watch. "What if I don't?"

"I'll put you in a large cardboard box and ship you by overnight mail," her mother replied patiently.

Luci wasn't convinced. She was certain the taxi driver hadn't understood which terminal was their destination.

A horn blared from another cab. The driver rolled down the window and shouted out a torrent of words in an incomprehensible language. Luci slid across the seat to her mother. "What if he takes us to Air Myanmar instead of Air France?" she whispered.

"The man's a professional. He does this every day."

The driver twisted backward in his seat to face them and smiled broadly. "Every day to airport. Seven years in America. Land of the free. Good job. Drive taxi. Not go home again. Stay here."

"Keep your eyes on the road!" Luci cautioned.

An airport shuttle cut in front of the cab and the driver shook his fist passionately at the windshield.

Stay here? Not likely. Luci wanted to travel. It didn't matter where she went, she wanted to go.

The driver brought the cab to a squealing halt in front of the terminal and raised both hands in a sign of triumph. Luci scrambled out, dragging her flight bag with her. She stood on the sidewalk as her mother paid the driver and took the suitcase.

Good-bye New York. Hello World.

They hurried into the terminal. People were rushing in every direction, toting huge parcels, dragging suitcases on wheels, pushing carts stacked with luggage.

"Gate Fourteen," Mrs. McKennitt determined after checking a television monitor. "You know I can't go to the gate and wait with you."

"I know." They walked swiftly down the concourse.

"You'll be all right."

Luci's stomach was beginning to flutter. She desperately wanted to see the world, know firsthand how other people lived, but now that she was moments away from departure, she felt a wave of uncertainty.

Getaway Tours had been created specifically to cater to the needs and interests of teenagers. Several times a year a small group traveled to unique and exciting locations around both the United States and the world. There would be none of the standard tourist traps for this company, which prided itself on its record of providing adventures for twenty-five years.

Over the past five weeks Luci had read and reread the brochures, studied the itineraries, envisioned the castles, mountains, and sparkling seas. She had memorized the biographies of the tour guides. Fran Atkinson was an adventurer herself who had met her freelance-photographer husband, Tim, when following the original route of the medieval pilgrims to Santiago de Compostela in Spain. Luci imagined how thrilling it would be to cross through France and Spain on foot and horseback just as the travelers did in the 1400s. Of all the tours and tour guides in the world, Fran was the one Luci felt would be right for her.

Luci faced the metal detector. No turning back now.

"You can call if you have any problems, but I'm sure you won't." Mrs. McKennitt kissed her daughter on the cheek. "Go have a wonderful time and—"

"Eat whole foods." Smiling, Luci finished the sentence for her mother. "Say good-bye to Dad."

"I will. See you in a week."

Luci placed her bag on the conveyor belt. Stepping through the metal detector, she was relieved when no sirens wailed because an X ray of her hairdryer looked suspicious.

Gate 14 seemed to be at least two miles down the concourse, past snack shops, magazine stands, and duty-free shops.

Did she need a magazine? What if the other tourists weren't friendly? She'd need something to do for six hours. What if she didn't know what to say to them? What if they didn't even speak English?

Luci pictured the group speaking in pidgin English when they were not using crude sign language to communicate.

Gate 14 was up ahead.

Luci saw someone leave the waiting area. The girl was tall, had skin the color of creme caramel, and seemed to have done absolutely nothing to control her unruly and completely enviable long dark hair. Everything she wore was standard issue but went perfectly together. Faded jeans, paddock boots. Was that a guy's shirt? Jean jacket. How did it look so good on her?

The girl disappeared down the concourse as Luci crossed into the waiting area and approached the hand-painted sign that announced Getaway Tours.

A sturdy young woman in her twenties greeted her warmly. "You must be Luci! I'm Fran Atkinson, your tour guide. This is Tim, my fellow traveler and husband."

Tim, who was in the process of fixing a strap on a camera bag, smiled broadly and held out his hand. "Welcome aboard."

Fran put her arm around Luci's shoulders. "I'm glad you made it."

Luci sighed. "Me, too."

Fran continued: "These evening flights can be a

little difficult, what with all the traffic. We've never lost anyone yet, though we seem to be short a few cohorts at the moment. Let me introduce you to the rest of the group. This is our contingent from California. Stacey Rush, who lives in Los Angeles . . ."

The auburn-haired, impeccably coiffed girl looked up from a fashion magazine. "Santa Monica," she corrected.

"And this is Daria Kenter from Peralta," Fran continued.

"Hi." The olive-skinned girl's smile came and went so fast Luci wasn't sure it had been there at all.

Fran took her a few steps farther down the row. Luci's eyes widened. Sitting alone on the last of the plastic seats was a pale girl with a spiky black crew cut, wearing earphones.

"This is Aimee Acacia." Fran waited for Aimee to reply, then touched her on the arm.

Aimee opened her eyes and slid one earphone back. Her pale skin was in stark contrast to her hair. She wore black leggings and a hugely oversized black T-shirt that was nearly falling off her thin shoulders.

"This is Luci McKennitt," Fran told Aimee.

"Really?"

"She's on the tour with us."

Aimee smiled, then pulled the earphone back on and went back to her alternative 'zine.

Fran turned to Luci. "It's Aimee's first tour, too. She's very . . . creative."

Luci nodded slowly. Learning about different lifestyles had started already.

"The flight should be boarding in about fifteen

minutes, so if there's anything anyone needs to do . . ."

Tim gave his flight bag a zip. "That's Fran's way of saying there aren't many gas stations or burger stands from here on."

Stacey looked up. "They are feeding us on this flight, aren't they?"

Fran smiled. "Many times."

"If I paid for food, I want food," Stacey replied.

Luci placed her bag near the only empty seat and sat down.

The tall girl Luci had seen leave the waiting area now reentered, dropped her jacket on the flight bag, and sat next to Luci. She pushed her hair back over her shoulder. "I'm Jay Hamilton."

"I'm Luci McKennitt. Have you been here long?"

"Yeah. I had to take a bus from Connecticut and wound up being the first to get here. Then those two showed up." Jay motioned toward Stacey and Daria. "And it's been a fashion show ever since. I started wondering who I had to name my first child after to get a single room."

"Can we choose who we room with?"

"I think so as long as it's not with one of the young gentlemen."

"There are guys?" Luci glanced around the waiting area.

"One headed down the concourse about ten minutes ago, but there's one more. He's cutting it close."

"How do you know?"

"Fran and Tim were wondering if one of them

should make arrangements to take the next flight if he didn't show up soon."

"Is this your first tour?"

"Yes. Yours?"

Luci nodded. "I've always wanted to travel, but my parents weren't convinced I was old enough or responsible enough."

"What changed their minds?"

"Nothing." Luci grinned. "After months of talking about it, I wore them down. It's my birthday present."

"Mine's a gift from a friend."

"You have a generous friend."

"Very."

Curiosity was getting the better of Luci. "You don't sound like you're from Connecticut."

"Montreal. My mother and I moved to Westport last year."

"Canada. That must be fascinating."

"Maybe so, but it's also strange."

Luci couldn't imagine how that could be possible. She'd seen photos of Montreal and it appeared to be a lovely city. "How so?"

"People acting like the language police, insisting that you speak French even if you're not a French Canadian. It's the law in Montreal."

Luci imagined furtive groups of criminals gathering in dark alleys and catacombs in order to speak English. "But the good part is that you must be bilingual." Luci conceded.

"Not since I got to America. I vowed I would never speak French again. At least not unless it's crucial."

Luci glanced around the waiting area. "What's with the one with the hair? Or without it."

"Aimee?" Jay shrugged. "She's been sitting there for the last hour. Her ears must be sweating by now."

"What's she listening to? Alternative rock?"

Jay dismissed this remark with a breath. "That's Paleolithic. She said it was cybermusic."

"What's that? Does it have something to do with computers?"

"It's the singing of one thousand computers when they get rid of us for the day."

"Seriously?"

"I don't have a clue what it is."

A voice on the public-address system announced that the flight would soon begin boarding. Throughout the waiting area, passengers began to gather up their belongings.

After instructing everyone to stay exactly where they were, Fran and Tim hurriedly searched up and down the concourse for the missing members of the group.

"What happens if a passenger doesn't make the flight?" Luci wondered.

"Maybe we'll find out," Jay replied as the first-class boarding call was announced and people began lining up at the passageway.

Luci collected her things and got in line behind Jay, thanking her lucky stars that the cabdriver had brought them to the right terminal. Being late for something this important would be too embarrassing for words.

Fran returned and began consulting with the ticket agent, trying to determine exactly how long it would be before the flight left. Tim got on the courtesy phone. His and Fran's concern had developed into full-blown worry.

"Someone goofed," Jay commented.

"Big time," Luci answered, clutching her ticket in her hand.

Two young men rushed into the waiting area. One had streaked blond hair, almost all one length, falling to his shoulders. The other had long, brown, very straight hair parted in the middle and he wore what appeared to be a hand-embroidered vest.

Luci couldn't take her eyes off him and leaned close to Jay. "Who is that?"

"That's Glin Woods. I don't know the other."

Fran breathed a sigh of relief as she caught sight of the young men. "Logan!"

"Made it. Got in a side door." Grinning, Logan didn't seem fazed by his late arrival.

"You have to go through the metal detector," Daria commented.

Logan caught a lock of hair between his fingers and pushed it out of his eyes. "Not if you have connections."

Tim ushered the two toward the line. "Did your father fly you in again?"

"All the way from Atlanta. Air Traffic Control tried to reroute us to Newark," Logan replied.

He turned and smiled when he saw Jay. Logan walked directly to her and held out his hand. "I'm Logan Carlisle."

"Jay Hamilton."

"This must be your first tour. If you have any questions . . ."

Jay nodded. "Fran will have all the answers. Thank you for pointing that out."

Jay handed her ticket to the woman at the entrance and was down the jetway in a split second. Luci hurried after her.

"He seemed to like you. Didn't you think he was cute?" she added.

Jay didn't slow her long stride. "You can't take these things too seriously. Lots of people are cute." She stopped at the door to the plane. "But I'm cute, too." There was a twinkle in her eye. They both burst into laughter.

The flight attendant greeted them and pointed toward their seats.

Jay squeezed past passengers stuffing raincoats and bags into overhead storage cabinets. "My mother has always been real clear about one thing. Guys can be handsome. They can be charming. They can even be endearing. But a girl must be a wise consumer."

"Turn them over and see if the other side isn't spoiled?"

"Exactly."

Luci thought about it. That was an unusual approach to interpersonal relationships.

"Window or aisle?" Jay asked.

"Trade halfway?"

"Deal." Jay slid her way to the window.

Luci squashed her flight bag under the seat and made herself as comfortable as possible in the small space. She glanced over to Jay and hoped they'd be able to room together. She wanted to get to know her better, learn about Montreal, and definitely understand Jay's theory about being a wise consumer. It seemed she knew much more about the whole subject than Luci did.

Logan came down the narrow aisle followed by Glin. Luci watched as they found seats several rows up from her own.

"Does that one fall under the heading of they can be handsome, they can be endearing?"

"Glin?" Jay regarded him thoughtfully. He was tall and slender, but not thin. His hair was the color of pecans, brown with hints of reddish gold, and it fell gracefully to his shoulders.

"Yes."

"Do you fancy him?" Jay asked.

Before Luci could reply that he was the best-looking guy she had ever seen, Stacey leaned over the seat from behind. "He looks like a fugitive from a Renaissance fair. Where'd he get those clothes?"

"I think the vest is great," Jay replied.

"For the Middle Ages," Stacey answered. "Huzzah!"

Glin turned to face her. Luci felt her face grow hot with embarrassment. Did he think she had called out to him? "Waes hael!" He waved at Stacey.

"What'd I tell you." Stacey plunked herself down.

Jay leaned over to Luci. "Is she going to follow us all the way to Europe?"

"Yes, unless the tail of the plane falls off into the Atlantic."

It was good that Glin and Logan were several rows

ahead of them. If they were across the aisle, Luci knew she'd be dropping food on her lap, spilling drinks, and getting herself tangled up in the seat belt. Forget about going to the lavatory. That would definitely have to wait for France.

"What's the movie?" Stacey asked no one in particular.

"Gobbledygook," Daria read from the inflight magazine. "The story of a family's hilarious Thanksgiving romp when their dinner is telecast live for a national audience. The holiday deteriorates when the ratings go down and two bumbling burglars are sent in to take the family hostage."

Luci pulled the seat belt snug. "Is that a documentary?"

Logan came over and knelt on the seat in front of them, facing backward. "Have you traveled before?"

Luci and Jay shook their heads.

"There are a few things you should remember. Don't exchange money on the street. It could be counterfeit. Counterfeiters get life imprisonment."

Luci's eyes opened wide.

Logan continued. "Keep all your receipts; you can get a refund on the taxes when you come home. It's called VAT—value added tax. Don't keep anything important in your backpack because pickpockets will target you. Don't eat any wild mushrooms. But you can drink the water anyplace in France. Except from those little green bottles. Very expensive."

An older gentleman stood in the aisle, coat in one hand, briefcase in the other. "Young man, may I take my seat?"

Fran pointed at Logan's assigned seat. "The welcoming committee will sit *now*."

"Fran," Logan began.

Tim came down the aisle. "Logan, I hear wing dining is all the rave. The best tables are in front of the jet wash. Of course you still need a big steel cable attached to your ankle to keep you from being swept off over Newfoundland. Would you like to try it?"

Undaunted, Logan smiled and went back to his seat.

"What a way to start a trip. Poisonous mushrooms and counterfeiters . . . ugh." Luci said. "What's next?"

"It sounds like good advice. I guess he's a seasoned traveler."

"Do you suppose he gives that same speech to all the girls?" Luci laughed.

"I hope not," Stacey said from the seat behind them.

Jay twisted a narrow gold ring on her finger. "I guess someone's staking out her territory."

Smiling, Luci settled back in the seat as the plane began to back away from the terminal.

This was going to be a good trip.

Chapter Two

"**I**ck." Luci put the fork down on her tray. "I thought airline food was supposed to have gotten better."

Jay stabbed her fork at the chicken Florentine on her miniature plate. "It's fighting me." She followed it around until she stopped the meat in the corner with her knife.

"You can't eat that tough thing."

"I can if I can get it to my mouth."

Luci tried the roll. "Margarine? Can't they use real butter?"

"Do you know how much real butter costs in Montreal?"

"No."

"About three dollars a pound."

"Wow. My mother would go broke in a month. She uses about two hundred pounds of butter a week."

"Doing what?" Jay asked in amazement. "Swimming in it?"

"She has a whole-foods catering business and a small retail store in Manhattan."

With a clatter of trays and silverware, Stacey stood up, straightened her clothes, and made her way down the aisle toward the lavatory.

"Why's she going to that lav when there's one right behind us?" Luci asked.

"Because the boys aren't behind us."

"Oh." That was something she would never have thought of. Luci folded her napkin neatly and placed it over her plate. It seemed best to put dinner out of its misery.

Several minutes later Stacey exited from the lavatory, makeup redone, unwrinkled and fresh, emerging like a photograph from *Elle*. Luci had to respect the girl for being able to retain her flawless exterior when the rest of the passengers on the plane resembled survivors of a clothing-store explosion.

Stacey strolled deliberately up the aisle. Her pace slowed considerably as she neared Glin and Logan. She seemed to lose her balance at that moment and had to put her hand out to steady herself. Luckily for her, Logan's shoulder was right there to be of assistance.

Logan looked up, smiled, and said something that couldn't be heard over the roar of the engines. Stacey returned his smile and replied.

Jay shook her head in amazement.

"How'd she do that?" Luci asked.

"Practice."

"Incredible."

"The maneuver was executed perfectly, but I take two points off the total score for obviousness."

Luci held up a fork like a microphone. "Yes, viewers, that was a fine performance by our California competitor, Stacey Rush, who exhibited enviable style and grace but lost points for being transparent. I'm sure we'll be seeing her make another attempt before the competition is over."

"Please stay tuned to this channel for more of the show *Target: Logan Carlisle*. And now a word from our sponsors . . ." Jay finished and she and Luci burst out laughing simultaneously.

The flight attendants soon collected all the trays and glasses in order for the movie to begin. Aimee passed on the film, since she was still wearing her headphones.

The lights were dimmed. The small screen was filled with a huge stuffed turkey wearing a pilgrim's hat and black, buckled shoes. The bird began to rumba in time to the music.

Luci and Jay watched the movie for a few minutes then became bored with the antics of the nerdy-father character and his family.

Jay found a miniature deck of cards in the pocket in front of her seat and held them out to Luci. "What do you play in America?"

"My grandmother always played fan-tan."

"Okay. Show me how."

Luci shuffled the cards.

"Where do you go to school?"

Luci dealt the cards. "A private school on the Upper

West Side. It's very traditional. We wear uniforms and we're expected to behave like ladies at all times."

Sometimes Luci almost felt like rebelling against all the rules, but the fact was, she didn't mind them except on rare occasions, and on the evenings when there was a dance. All the girls had instructions to sit primly with their ankles crossed underneath their chairs and not to fidget. Luci couldn't help but fidget with the result that she was always writing papers about comportment and genteel behavior during her detentions.

The music at the dances tended to be oversupervised and to feature too many inappropriate musical groups (Poison, Megadeth). Any jewelry containing spikes was prohibited, but since Luci didn't want to wear anything that seemed as though it had originally been designed for a dog, she could hardly complain passionately about that rule.

Jay picked up her cards. "In Montreal, my school was so exclusive that you practically had to give them your pedigree to get in."

"No kidding." Luci had heard of such schools, but hers was certainly not one of them.

Jay studied her cards for a moment. "Educationally it was the best, but the administrators were snobs. If they weren't being forced to balance out the student body with members of the peasant class, they would never have accepted me."

Luci imagined a snowstorm and Jay in rags, holding out a tin cup trying to earn pennies to attend the huge castlelike school. The rich kids with their pedigrees would come up to the gate in stretch limos and toss her pencil stubs.

"You must have hated it."

"Not at all. I'm very grateful I had the opportunity to get that kind of education. I think I was doing them a favor, too."

"How?"

"By being someone they wouldn't normally meet."

That made sense to Luci. "We're just regular kids at my school. Except there is one girl who's a princess."

"A real one or just a brat?"

"A real one. She's okay, though." Luci put down a card. "Where do you go to school now?"

"In Westport. I like it. You can see the Sound from the back lawn. My mother would never be able to afford to send me to my new school, but the woman who owns the antique shop where she works has rather adopted us. She's offered to send me to school and she's sending me on this trip."

"Oh, that's why you said she was a very nice friend."

"Lily's the least selfish person I've ever met. Her mother made a fortune in hats."

Luci studied the cards in her hand. "Maybe someday my mother will make a fortune in croutons. That's one of her specialties."

"Does she make anything else?"

"Lots of things. A great chocolate cake. Apple pie. A nitrite-free ham casserole with pears and onions."

"Do you know how to cook?"

"I wouldn't have been able to avoid it. I help at the store after school and on weekends. Not all the time. It's fun."

"Is it a big store?"

Luci laughed. "About as big as a broom closet. You get three people inside and two of them are waiting on the street. My mother does a good take-out business. People who work late, and don't want to come home to cook, stop by and pick something up. But it's better than pizza or frozen dinners because it's real food."

"What do you eat for dinner?"

"Oh, you mean, is it like the shoemaker whose kids go barefoot?"

"Something like that."

"Do I look like I'm starving?"

"No."

"I have a policy. If I'm going to eat something, it has to be worth it. I'm not eating tortilla chips or plastic-filled cupcakes."

"Plastic?"

"All those creme fillings are nondairy. Well, if they're not dairy, what are they? Petroleum products?"

"I never thought about it that way."

"It's how I was raised."

Jay put down her last card. "What do you say when you win?"

Luci scrutinized the cards. Jay had won. She shrugged in bewilderment. No one had ever discussed cheering during this game. "Nah-nah?"

Smiling, Jay gathered the cards to deal another hand.

"It's funny, considering how you feel about speaking French, that you're going to southern France."

"I don't have anything against France. But I'm not going there to translate for everyone. You guys are on your own."

"Great. *Donnez-moi la baguette*. Asking for bread should get me a long way on the subway. Do they have subways?"

"I think it said in the guidebook there's one in Toulouse. How long are we expected to stay there?"

"One night, I think. But the itinerary is supposed to be very flexible."

Getaway Tours operated much like a democracy. If the tourists wanted to make changes to the original plan, that was acceptable—provided arrangements could be made. Travel was usually by a rented van, so they rarely had to depend on mass-transit schedules or the desires of a larger group. Small hotels could often accommodate the arrival of ten or twelve people at one time with more ease than a larger hotel whose business concentrated on the tourist trade.

"I don't know much more about Languedoc than I read in the brochure," Jay admitted. "It's in the foothills of the Pyrenees. I'm sure it's scenic, but why is this such an appealing tourist destination? And if it's so interesting, why don't more people go there the way they go to the Côte d'Azur?"

"Maybe they haven't heard of it. Languedoc was once a very important region of France. During the Middle Ages, it was much more culturally and educationally advanced than most of Europe. Because of the ports, it was a trading center for the Mediterranean. Because of the warm climate, it was favorable for agriculture."

"How did you get so smart?"

Luci laughed. "I went to the library as soon as I was booked on the tour. I memorized all of that."

Someone behind them tapped on their seat. "Why don't you shut off the light so the rest of us can sleep?" Stacey asked.

Jay turned toward her. "Because then we wouldn't be able to see the cards in the dark, and I don't read braille."

"You'll look like hell in the morning," Stacey replied, and pulled her blanket around her.

Jay raised an eyebrow and let the remark pass as she and Luci began another game.

Sunlight was streaming in the small windows. Passengers were rubbing their eyes and trying to work out the kinks their bodies had developed during the night.

"Did you two talk all night?" Fran asked as she crouched by their seats the next morning. She fluffed her short hair and it fell into place.

"Just about," Jay said.

"When we get to Toulouse, we'll go directly to the hotel. It's something of a free day, so if you want to take a nap, you can."

"What if we don't want to nap?" Luci asked.

"Tim and I are splitting to go in two different directions. One will probably be shopping, the other will be sightseeing."

"I know who'll want to go shopping," Jay commented.

"We aim to please. Toulouse is really quite an attractive city. It's known as *la ville rose*—the pink city—because there were no quarries from which to get marble. Most of the buildings are built from rose-colored brick. Tonight we'll all gather for dinner and then go to a jazz club."

Luci smiled. This is exactly what she had hoped for. Trying everything. "Sounds like fun."

"What about the room assignments?" Jay asked.

"It's up to you. This isn't summer camp." Fran stood. "I guess you two have already decided."

Luci and Jay nodded.

"Good," Fran replied, and continued down the aisle. She stopped to speak with Logan and Glin.

A voice came over the intercom just then. "*Bonjour.* Good morning. I am Captain Patrick Plévin. We should be landing at the Aeroport International de Toulouse-Blagnac in twenty minutes. The weather today in Toulouse is clear, the temperature will be twenty-five degrees."

Luci looked to Jay.

"That's centigrade," Jay reminded her.

"Phew."

"About seventy-five degrees Fahrenheit."

"That'll be nice."

The captain resumed his speech. "I hope you've enjoyed your flight and will fly with us again."

Luci glanced across the aisle. Aimee was sitting as she had been since the beginning of the flight, earphones on, reading.

"Have you spoken to her?" Luci asked Jay.

"No. Does she talk?"

"She said hi to me."

"That's good to know. She has acquired speech. Do you know anything about her?"

"Nothing."

"She wouldn't get into my school."

Luci checked out the black nail polish covering Aimee's ultra-short nails. "Mine either."

"Ladies and gentlemen, may I have your attention," a flight attendant's voice came over the intercom. "There seems to be a traffic problem at the airport. Our scheduled landing will be delayed. Please make yourselves comfortable until further notice."

Luci sighed impatiently. "Great. Now that I'm here, I can't get down."

"There's something wrong. That's bull, if I've ever heard it," Logan said loudly enough for Luci to hear.

Luci leaned forward in her seat. "What do you mean?"

Logan turned to her. "It's a clear day. It's first thing in the morning. There's not that much traffic. Did anyone hear the landing gear go down?"

Stacey gasped. "The landing gear is broken?"

"No one said that," Glin replied.

"No one had to!"

Jay put a hand on Luci's arm. "Don't listen to him. What makes him an authority? Some plane on the ground probably had a flat tire or an applecart tipped over."

"Yeah, you're probably right. The worst never happens."

"What planet are you from?" Stacey asked. "The worst happens all the time."

Luci thought about it. Stacey was right. "Look at it this way, Stacey; you're in no danger of an earthquake now."

"I'll take comfort in that thought. Once I get on the ground."

Daria dashed down the aisle. "I was just up in first class. We can't land!"

Chapter Three

Fran rose and went to Daria. "Slow down. Relax. Take a deep breath. What are you talking about?"

The expression of sheer panic on Daria's face didn't subside as she tried to catch her breath. "I was forward, trying to see what first class looked like and I overheard two flight attendants talking. They said there's a problem with the landing gear and we can't land!"

"That's impossible. We don't have the fuel to stay airborne much longer," Logan said.

"Enough logistics, Logan," Tim ordered.

"I didn't pack a parachute," Luci said.

"If we work real fast, maybe we can tie some Kleenex together," Jay replied.

Stacey kicked their seats. "Stop it! Can't they crank the gear down?"

"We'll probably have to ditch in the Med." Logan remained remarkably calm.

Stacey was growing more fevered. "Do these planes float?"

"Like a safe," Logan said.

Tim reached forward and put his hand over Logan's mouth.

"This is just great. The first time I get to travel and we can't land. Next time I'm taking the train," Luci told Jay.

"If we listen to Logan, there won't be a next time."

"Does that mean it's too late to get a refund?" Luci teased.

"Yes, it's too late. We're doomed!" Daria cried.

Fran clapped her hands together. "We're not doomed! We're not going to swim to shore and we're not going to scare ourselves! Come on, guys. This is supposed to be an adventure!"

"A little too much adventure, I'd say," Stacey remarked.

"The whole world isn't a sterilized, sanitized amusement park like Walt Disney World," Tim told them.

"Which is looking pretty good right about now," Stacey shot back.

"None of you wanted to go to Florida. You asked for Getaway Tours. You got it. Now . . . let's enjoy the experience!" Fran told them cheerfully.

"Does she believe that?" Jay asked Luci.

"The scary part is, I think she does."

Fran patted Luci on the shoulder as she went back to her seat.

"Maybe we should tell Aimee," Daria said.

Everyone in the group looked at Aimee, who was happily listening to her music, reading contentedly, blissfully unaware.

"Nah."

Pulling the emergency instructions from the pocket in front of her, Luci studied it. Uh-huh, take the seat apart and hold on to it in case the plane goes down in the water. Luci hoped there was a lot of salt in the Mediterranean, because she didn't think she was a strong enough swimmer to make it to Gibraltar.

"Has anyone taken a class in lifesaving techniques?" Luci asked.

Glin turned in his seat to look at her. "I have."

Luci smiled weakly. Of course, it would have been him. Don't make a fool of yourself, Luci, she thought. "Do you have any suggestions?"

"Well, if we're going into the water, we should all strip." Glin smiled. "Clothes will just weigh you down."

Luci closed her eyes.

Jay leaned over to her. "Stop while you're ahead."

"I'm not ahead," she whispered.

"I know," Jay whispered back.

"Ladies and gentlemen, may I have your attention please," a flight attendant's voice announced the intercom. "We will be landing at Toulouse-Blagnac in ten minutes. Due to some difficulties we will be landing . . ."

"Where? In a field?" Logan asked.

"Shhh!" Daria hissed.

". . . on the runaway and disembarking there. Buses will be provided. Please make sure your seats are in the upright position. Thank you for your patience."

"That's good, right?" Jay said.

"Right," Luci replied. "We don't have to swim and we don't have to walk."

Soon the plane was making its descent. The city of Toulouse, with its many red-tiled roofs, was visible beneath the wings and Luci's heart quickened. It was all coming true. In just minutes she'd be on foreign ground.

The flight attendants rapidly moved up the aisles, checking to see if the carry-on bags were stowed and the passengers' seat belts were tight.

The roar from the engines deepened and the plane was nosed downward. Closer and closer the ground seemed to rise until there was a bump and a squeal. The landing gear had descended. They had landed.

The plane slowly taxied to the end of the runway, where several buses were parked nearby.

The air stairs were backed up to the aircraft's door and the flight attendants proceeded down the aisle, one row at a time, helping the passengers leave the plane. There was no talking, no music, no sound except the engines winding down.

Jay and Luci gathered their things together and then trailed behind the flight attendant to the door. They stepped out into the bright sunshine. Luci had trouble adjusting to all the light with the sun shining in her eyes.

"Down the stairs and onto the bus," a flight attendant instructed.

Luci stepped off the platform. As she was about to take another step she realized her flight bag was caught on something and gave it a firm tug. It didn't give immediately, then, when it did, it caught Luci off balance. She attempted to get her feet under her but missed the next step.

Down she went. Rolling, tumbling, and bouncing to the ground below.

Air knocked out of her, Luci struggled to catch her breath. She raised her eyes. An airport security guard was staring down at her, then motioned toward the bus.

Jay and Glin raced down the stairs to her side.

Glin knelt beside her. "Are you okay?"

Jay grabbed Luci's arm. "Don't try to talk. You're okay. You're okay. Just get on the bus!"

With Glin holding one arm and Jay holding the other, Luci was nearly dragged down the gauntlet of armed men lining the path to the bus. She was plunked into a seat while still trying to get her breath.

"Is anything broken?" Jay asked.

"I don't think so."

"This is a story you can tell your grandchildren," Jay pointed out practically.

Glin slid into the seat behind them. "Do you think you need to see a doctor?"

Logan sat next to him. "If she didn't lose consciousness, she's fine. You don't need to go to some French hospital, do you?"

It was obvious that Logan would consider her an enormous wimp if she admitted to any weakness or frailty.

Luci shook her head and closed her eyes. No

doctors. Not unless they could cure her of deep and permanent embarrassment.

The Hotel Poussin was located on a tree-lined side street. The concierge had them all shown to their rooms, which were small but pleasant. A wail came from down the hallway when Stacey learned that each room had a sink with running water, but the rest of the facilities were communal.

"Do you expect me to . . ." she began.

Jay motioned to Luci as she stuck her head out the door. "We have to hear this."

Luci came to the door. Logan and Glin had their door open as well.

Fran stood in front of Stacey patiently. "Expect you to what?"

"Share . . . sit . . ." Stacey was floundering her words.

"This is Europe," Fran pointed out.

"I understand that, but good taste . . . sanitary considerations would suggest . . ." Stacey sighed.

Fran was all compassion. "Yes, Stacey, you share the toilet with everyone else."

Stacey gathered her dignity and raised her chin decisively. "I'm putting paper down."

Fran patted her shoulder. "Do whatever it takes." She turned, not even trying to contain her smile.

"Geezel," Jay said. "She thinks we're all walking biohazards! My rump's as good as hers any day."

Logan and Glin nodded in agreement from their doorway.

Jay regarded them evenly, not giving them the satisfaction of a reply.

Daria raced from the lavatory holding a long strip of shiny toilet paper. "Stacey! You're not going to believe this stuff!"

Jay stepped back into the room and closed the door.

"Did your mother tell you to pack paper?" Luci asked.

"No."

Luci held out a roll. "Mine did."

"Let's not share it with her."

"Deal."

Luci continued unpacking the clothes and toiletries she would need for the afternoon and evening. Pants, a shirt, a sweater if the temperature dropped later on. Her wardrobe was simple, utilitarian. Nothing like she imagined Stacey's would be.

"Did you see that sweater Stacey threw on her Gucci bag?"

"The one that must have cost five hundred dollars?" Jay replied.

"It was beautiful. Everything she's wearing is top-of-the-line."

"Like that blue-faced Rolex watch."

"I don't think she bought that from a guy on the street."

Jay sat in an overstuffed chair. "Tell me about Santa Monica. That's where she's from, right? I don't know anything about it."

Luci sat on the edge of her bed. "It's on the ocean. A lot of television shows are filmed on the beach."

"Do you suppose her parents are famous or something?"

"That's probably a good guess. She seems pretty—I don't want to say spoiled."

"You don't think she's spoiled?"

"Of course, but I don't want to *say* it."

Jay put her feet up on the wastebasket. "When I see people like Stacey, I try to imagine what their lives are like. How much they have and how much they take for granted."

"People like that are usually pretty sheltered from the real world," Luci agreed. "I come from a normal family. We have some nice things, but no house in the Hamptons, no limousine waiting to take us across town. My parents are great people. I have no complaints."

"None?"

"I know that sounds weird. I guess I'm one of those few individuals who doesn't come from a dysfunctional family."

"I think my circumstances are probably a hundred and eighty degrees away from Stacey's. My mother's my best friend, always has been, but we've never had much money to spare."

"Where's your father?"

"After the divorce, when I was four, he went back to Jamaica."

"Oh," Luci said, the realization dawning on her. "I was wondering."

"Wonder no more. My mother's white, my father's black. He went home and is making tons of money selling souvenirs to the tourists."

"You can make a ton of money doing that?"

"He's a great businessman. He's got a chain of gewgaw shops all over the island."

"And doesn't send you any money?"

"No, and I wouldn't take it even if he did." Jay stood and went to her suitcase. "I don't have any need for someone who's incapable of having genuine feelings." She removed a colorful quilted vest from her suitcase and held it up. "Do you think this would be good for tonight?"

Luci couldn't help reaching out to touch the garment. "It's lovely. Where did you get it?"

"My mother made it. She manages a shop that sells antique quilts. Sometimes they have holes in them or are badly frayed or stained with age. You can cut them apart and turn the good sections into pillows or vests or maybe a skirt. At least then it doesn't go to waste."

"I'm sure it's more precious than anything Stacey could buy."

Jay smiled. "Just for that, you've made a friend for life."

It was soon discovered that Stacey needed to go shopping immediately. She had to buy great quantities of a rare perfume called Décadence that wasn't sold in America. Too expensive for public consumption, it was so far beyond the nose of the average person that the manufacturer restricted its sale.

Stacey was an authority on Décadence. Pronounced in the French way. She knew everything about this scent down to the ingredients, which were all natural. The special rose oil used in the perfume cost $5,000 an ounce because the flower petals were collected in Bulgaria by hand. If machinery was used, the petals would be bruised and the fragrance would be compromised.

Other, lesser perfumes used synthetics. Those scents were created in a laboratory. Décadence was created fresh from the field, so exclusive the container couldn't be ordinary glass. The bottle was Lalique crystal.

As Stacey was raving about this perfume Luci couldn't help suspecting that it was the kind of aroma that would threaten to make passengers in an elevator keel over before they reached their floor.

Luci had no regrets that she wouldn't be going along on the shopping junket with Stacey and Daria. She hadn't come all the way to France to stay inside a store.

Instead, Tim took the rest of the group on a sightseeing excursion beginning at the Place du Capitole, the city's main square. They strolled on to the Vieux Quartier, the old quarter. The route was closed to motor vehicles, so they were able to freely enjoy the shops and places of interest. At noon, they decided on a sidewalk café, passing up the opportunity to eat Américain and partake of un Big Mac at "McDo's." However, there were *pommes frites,* a bistro specialty, for those who couldn't miss French fries.

As they ate, Tim read casually from a guidebook. "Toulouse was a Visigoth capital fifteen hundred years ago. If you're forgetting your history, the Visigoths were a Teutonic tribe which swept through what's now Europe and made everyone fairly unhappy."

"That would include the Italians," Glin interjected, "since the Visigoths sacked Rome."

Tim nodded. "The book says they remained quite the warriors and successfully defended Toulouse against the Muslims in 721."

"More wars, more fighting," Luci said as she reached for a slice of crispy potato.

Tim continued. "In the Middle Ages there was no country of France as we know it now. The northern part of Gaul spoke the *langue d'oil*. The southern part spoke *langue d'oc*. The region became known as Languedoc or Occitania.

"In the twelfth century the greatest ruler of Gaul was the Count of Toulouse, who controlled the region to the border of Italy. It was the most civilized part of Western Europe, blending strains of Roman, Jewish, and Arab influences, trading with the Levant."

"Europe was hardly the most sophisticated region in the world at the time. It was really something of a dark age compared to the Arab world," Glin commented.

"In what way?" Jay asked.

"The Arabs had medicine. Real medicine, not the attach-leech, drain-blood, watch-patient-die-of-blood-loss variety. They had astronomy. The scientific names of stars are still in Arabic," Glin explained. "They had dual-entry bookkeeping."

"Languedoc enjoyed both financial security, a rich cultural life, and a strong independent spirit," Tim said as he continued reading the book. "The wealth in the region attracted many greedy men over the centuries and the independent spirit led to one of the greatest human slaughters in history." He closed the book and put it aside.

Luci looked up. "What did I miss?"

"The Inquisition started here," Glin said.

Jay pushed her plate away and leaned on the table. "Wasn't the Church of Rome going after a group of heretics? Some kind of witch-hunt."

"It was hardly that. The Cathars, as these people were known, were good Christians. At least that's what the pope's emissary reported back to him," Tim replied.

"Then what was the problem?" Logan asked.

"I'm no authority on the Cathars, but from what I know, some might say that for those days they were a little too good. In the Middle Ages, it was rather wild and woolly in the church. Priests and bishops weren't always as pious as the rules might have suggested. But in Languedoc, the Cathars were very strict and very spiritual."

Glin smiled. "Mark Twain said there's nothing people hate more than a good example. It sounds like that applied here."

"Another bone of contention may well have been that the Cathars had female priests."

"Good for them," Jay put in.

"Pope Innocent the Third ordered a crusade. Simon de Montfort mobilized a massive army to clean up the region once and for all. Men, women, and children, none were to be spared. I think the Cathars were outnumbered fifteen to one."

"Did that happen here in Toulouse?"

"No, actually the Cathars were located in several

other cities—Carcassonne, Béziers, Quéribus, Mont-segur."

"Is there anything left to see?"

"I believe so. The fortress of Montsegur still exits. It's high on a mountaintop, and it's possible to go through the ruins where the Cathars hid during the siege. Carcassonne is a beautiful medieval city. As a matter of fact, Kevin Costner filmed part of his movie *Robin Hood* there."

"Is Carcassonne on the itinerary?"

"No," Tim replied.

"Could it be?"

"If enough of you want to make the trip. It's not far."

"I vote for the side trip."

Jay tapped Aimee on the arm and she pulled back an earphone. "Do you want to go to Carcassonne?"

Aimee smiled and nodded as everyone raised their hands in agreement.

"Five for," Logan said. "That's a majority."

Chapter Four

"**W**here?" Stacey asked across the dinner table.

"Carcassonne," Luci said.

"What for?"

"To learn about the Cathars," Jay replied.

"Who are they?" Daria asked.

"A religious group," Logan explained.

Stacey swirled the ice in her glass. "Like monks?"

"No."

"Like the people who only wear black and make quilts? There was that movie about them . . . *Witness*. Harrison Ford was really good in that. The scene in the barn where they dance. What were they called?" Daria asked.

"The Amish," Stacey supplied.

"No . . . the Cathars weren't like the Amish," Luci told her.

Stacey was growing impatient. "Like Scientology? Dianetics? Theosophy? The Temple of Ma'at?"

"I don't think so," Luci admitted.

"What do they believe in?" Stacey asked irritably.

"Well, nothing now. They're dead," Glin finished.

"And you want to sabotage our trip for a bunch of dead people? They're not even around to produce a great wine, so I can bring a bottle home to my father. I don't think so."

"There are a group of monks in Canada who make a wonderful cheese called Oka," Jay said.

"I know," Luci replied. "I love it!"

"You can get it in America?"

"Oh sure. My mother uses it as an appetizer on a cheese platter. It holds its shape much better than Brie after a couple of hours on a buffet table."

Stacey dropped her fork with a clatter. "We're supposed to go to Saint-Tropez, not to see the remains of some weird cult. I thought we wanted to swim in the Mediterranean."

That was true. Back in New York, Luci had thought she wanted to swim in the Mediterranean, but now that she was sitting at the same table with Stacey, she wasn't so sure. She could imagine what Stacey would look like in the kind of bathing suit worn in Saint-Tropez and it gave her the beginnings of a dull headache. The kind no aspirin could cure.

French swimsuits were clothing only in theory. The hardware store had bigger strings than what tied those microchips of fabric together. It would have been different if there had been no guys on the trip. But the presence of Glin and Logan changed everything.

Luci looked across the table to Glin as he pushed some hair back over his shoulder. "Actually it's been put to a vote. Five for. What sayest thou?" he said.

Stacey grimaced. "It looks like we're outvoted already. What's in it for us if I don't get to go shopping on the Côte d'Azur?"

"What are you on this trip for? We're supposed to have new experiences, adventures, fun," Logan said.

"I'm not," Daria commented. "I was sent on the trip for punishment."

No one said a word.

Luci didn't look up to see what anyone else's reaction was. Then the moment was broken by the young man serving dinner and they began to eat.

Still no one spoke.

Luci was trying to imagine how a European holiday could be a punishment, and if it was true, what kind of parents did Daria have? And what on earth were they punishing her for?

"How is your cassoulet, Luci?" Fran asked.

"I think the flavors would be well-balanced if the chef hadn't been so heavy-handed with the rosemary." From a lifetime of living with gourmet cuisine, Luci spoke without thinking.

"Who are you? The Brutal Gourmet?" Stacey fairly snarled.

Luci's mind went blank. She couldn't think of anything to say. Here it was the first night out and she'd already made a fool of herself. It was bad enough to have taken a header down the jet steps. She hadn't recovered from that yet and now she'd just done it again.

Logan clinked his fork onto his plate. "Now that you mention it, I think there are too many parsnips in mine."

"And there's too much thyme in mine," Glin added.

Jay put down her fork. "There's too much food in mine."

The silence hung in the air.

Fran dabbed at her lips with her napkin. "Right. Let's talk about the change in plans for a moment. We can still get to Saint-Tropez. Carcassonne's only one night."

"Exactly what is in Carcassonne?" Stacey snapped.

"A medieval walled city," Glin replied.

"Anything else?" Daria asked.

"It's very pretty," Fran said.

"I take it you're leaving out all the other fantastic things to see and do there." When there was no reply, Stacey pursed her lips. "I thought so. Next time it'd be nice if we were asked before the vote was taken."

Luci had to admit to herself that Stacey had a point. She wouldn't have been very happy if everyone had decided to change the itinerary completely and then announce it as a fait accompli.

What would make it better for Stacey? "Kevin Costner was there, right, Fran?"

"Big deal," Stacey commented. "Costner's last movies have barely made back their investment."

"Says who?" Tim asked.

Stacey flounced her shoulders as if the answer was apparent. *"Daily Variety."*

"Bien sûr," Jay murmured, and exchanged a knowing glance with Luci.

*   *   *

They walked along le Quai de Tounis and admired the city lights and the rounded arches of the Pont-Neuf reflected in the waters of the Garonne River. Continuing their stroll, Tim made a firm suggestion that they stay together since they would be passing through an area that thrived primarily at night and was none of their business.

That announcement got everyone's attention. Signs announcing dancing girls flashed neon, and they all made an attempt to catch a quick peek inside when a door swung open. Except for Stacey, who commented that Sunset Strip in Los Angeles was much more racy.

Jay wanted to know exactly what constituted the heightened raciness Stacey had referred to, since she had limited knowledge of California.

Stacey shook her head. "You have to understand Los Angeles is a magnet for people with more dreams than talent. More body than brains. More energy than motivation."

"Okay. And then what happens?" Jay asked.

"They crash and burn," she replied, and wouldn't elaborate further.

Jay fell back to walk alongside Luci. "The definitive description."

"From an authority," Luci agreed.

Glin took Logan's arm and pulled him away from the doorway to a club. "What kind of life do you think Stacey lives out in California?"

"One of privilege," Luci replied.

"Then how would she know about the bad part of town?"

"Everyone knows how sleazy the Strip is. You don't have to be from L.A."

"I didn't know."

"You're undoubtedly suffering from media deprivation."

"What's your recommendation?"

"Sit next to me at the club," Logan replied as he caught up to them. "I can answer all your questions. Solve all your problems. And put a smile on your face while I'm doing it."

Jay didn't smile. "I can do all that for myself, thank you very much."

Logan lifted his collar. "Brrr. Is that a cold front moving through?"

Stacey paused to look in a shop window and, as they neared, turned suddenly and bumped into Logan.

"Pardonnez-moi," Stacey told him. *"Parlez-vous français?"*

Luci and Jay walked faster up the street, leaving Logan behind. "Someone should be taking notes. We're seeing a master perform."

Luci felt like a kindergartner compared with Stacey, who seemed like a Ph.D. in dealing with the opposite sex. Stacey had a practiced air about her. She knew what to say and what to do.

Luci hadn't had any practice. There were boys in her school and she was friends with many of them, but they had never been more than friends. She couldn't even say she'd ever had a crush on anyone. That was probably a developmental deficit at her age.

"Backward," Luci said to herself.

"What is?" Jay asked.

Startled, Luci hadn't realized she had spoken aloud. "Me. I feel . . . socially inept."

"I doubt it."

"Wait till you know me a little better before you make a decision."

"I can draw accurate conclusions pretty fast."

That didn't surprise Luci at all.

"How many suitcases did Stacey bring?" Jay asked, changing the subject, and for that, Luci was grateful.

"Four."

"Then she is going to change outfits three times a day," Jay moaned.

They stopped to window-shop for a moment. "That'd be my guess."

Jay shrugged.

Luci glanced at Jay's midcalf full black skirt, simple shirt, and quilted vest. "That's a great look you've got. You seem put together . . . properly."

"It's the French influence. French women know how to dress. They choose black. It goes with everything and it doesn't require a lot of thought. One good skirt will go further than ten trendy outfits that go out of style before you reach the cash register."

They both watched Stacey as she walked on ahead. She was wearing an expensive outfit topped with a rose silk unconstructed jacket. Stacey did it justice. It was as though her clothes had just come off the rack, dressers had designed her look, and makeup artists had done her face. All that was required was a small push and she'd be ready to hit the runway at a fashion house.

"It's an entirely different way of thinking."

"Uh-huh."

Tim held the door open for the group and they entered the jazz cellar, going down the narrow stone steps into the low-ceilinged club. Dark and smoky, with dim yellow lights on every small table, it was already crowded. The group found their way to a corner and pushed two tables together, borrowing chairs from a table where a young woman and a young man were holding hands and wouldn't be needing any company.

Luci pulled back a chair for herself near the wall and Jay sat next to her. Logan quickly positioned himself so he was sitting by Jay. Glin was going to sit in the chair to Logan's right but caught himself before sitting on Stacey's lap. She pulled the chair closer to Logan. So close, the leg of her chair bumped into the leg of his chair.

Logan looked at her, then at Glin, who was grinning.

With all Stacey's maneuvering, Luci was finding herself crushed into the corner, little room under the table for her legs. She tried moving back, but the wall was too close. She put her purse on her lap and hoped the music would take her attention away from the close quarters. Luci had never been particularly fond of tight spaces.

A small stage had been built at the front of the room, only a few feet higher than the audience level. There were no curtains to hide the red brick wall, no special lighting, just a few microphones and a piano.

Fran had translated the poster they had seen outside the club. It was retro night and the band was playing music from Paris in the 1920s. A stylishly dressed young woman in a satin dress came up to the microphone and began singing.

Fran reached over and removed Aimee's headphones. "You can have it back in half an hour."

Aimee shrugged amiably.

Soon the group was applauding enthusiastically after each number.

The band took a break and Logan leaned toward Jay. "Have you ever been to a jazz club before?"

"Yes."

Glin leaned over the table. "Do you like jazz?"

Jay nodded.

"What about you, Luci?"

"Some. Some I just don't get."

Logan pushed his empty cola bottle to the middle of the table. "Glin's father's a musician. Glin is, too, but he rarely admits to it."

"Really?"

Glin nodded. "Yes, my father is a musician, and no, I do not admit to being anywhere near as talented as he is."

"What does he play?"

"Almost every instrument, but mostly the guitar. My father is in a trio which sings traditional folk songs and sea chanties."

"To the top of the charts with a bullet," Stacey commented.

Glin smiled agreeably. "There's no fame or fortune. It's a commitment to keep something alive which would otherwise be lost."

"I suppose they play at Renaissance fairs, too," Stacey continued.

"Not anymore, but it has happened."

"What did I tell you?" Stacey said under her breath.

Jay leaned over. "So, Stacey, did you get your perfume?"

Luci tapped Jay under the table. She didn't want to hear about the perfume.

"Only one bottle," Stacey complained.

"Isn't that enough? Perfume doesn't last forever. How much can you use?" Jay said.

"I have people who are expecting me to bring them back a present."

"Get them a statue of the Eiffel Tower," Tim suggested.

"Hardly. My best friend would be very disappointed. Ariel Fontaine?" Stacey looked around the table to see if anyone recognized the name. No one did. "She's an actress. And so beautiful. Without trying."

Aimee smiled. "A thing of beauty cannot be ignored."

"I recognize that," Tim said. "It's Percy Bysshe Shelley. No. No. It's John Keats. I'm really good at identifying poetry."

"It's the Hothouse Flowers," Aimee replied.

"Uh-huh." Stacey pushed back her chair. "Does anyone want to go to the ladies' room?"

Daria nodded, stood, and they both departed.

Logan looked up. "Why do women do that?"

Tim sighed. "You're asking one of the great unanswerable questions of the universe."

"Is their sense of direction so bad they can't find the can without help?" Logan couldn't be stopped.

"Is it loneliness?" Glin asked.

Fran laughed. "It's not about either. It's about sharing your thoughts with a friend in private."

"Are they talking about us in there?" Tim asked.

"They're doing their hair," Fran said.

"Doing their lipstick," Jay interjected.

"Blush," Luci added.

"Sounds tribal," Glin offered. "A ritual of applying war paint."

"It's more about bonding," Fran offered.

"Yeah, something like guys in the locker room all slapping each other on the butts and grunting," Jay remarked.

"I don't get it," Glin admitted.

"Well, when Stacey asked if anyone wanted to go, you should have gone to see what it was like," Luci said.

"If you ask," Glin said, "maybe I'll just do it."

Jay gave her a nudge under the table. "Come on, girlfriend," she said, loud enough for only Luci to hear.

Everyone waited for Luci's reply.

She looked Glin directly in the eye. "Wouldn't bother me, but I can't say it would help your reputation any."

Logan punched the air. "Good one!"

Jay and Luci exchanged a high five and everyone at the table laughed.

Luci lay in her bed that night, unable to sleep. Toulouse might have sounded like New York, but it smelled like Europe. The sheets, the towels, the water, the soap all smelled foreign.

"Are you still awake?" Jay asked softly.

"Yes."

"I'm glad you're my roommate."

"I was going to say the same thing, but I didn't want to sound like an idiot," Luci admitted.

"We should be able to say anything to each other."

"That's a deal."

There was a long pause. "I think Logan is interested in me."

"I think so, too. He's very attractive. Smart."

"Ummm."

"Is that a problem?"

"Yeah."

Luci waited a long time for Jay to say something else, but she didn't and finally Luci fell asleep.

Chapter Five

"**I**n the 700s, the Lady Carcas was the widow of Balac, the last Saracen governor of the city. This was a very attractive jewel that the Frankish king Charlemagne wanted to add to his crown. He laid siege to the city, but Lady Carcas and the citizens put up an incredible defense."

The group stood outside the Cité looking up at the fortress as the tour guide spoke in clear but accented English.

Luci's imagination filled in all the blanks in the guide's speech. She could almost hear the soldiers, undoubtedly standing where she was standing right now. The barbicans would have been flying banners, there would have been soldiers at the keeps. The drawbridge would have been raised.

"After five years the food had nearly run out and the people were losing hope. They looked to the good Lady Carcas for hope and inspiration. She decided to feed the last of the grain not to the starving people but to the remaining pig. Her people thought she might have lost her senses. Then she ordered for the bloated pig to be hurled over the battlements. Without resistance, her command was followed. Over the top of the wall the pig went, bursting like a bomb on the soldiers below."

"Ugh," Stacey said with a grimace.

"It makes you think twice about ordering scrapple for breakfast, doesn't it?" Logan grinned.

"I don't eat breakfast," Stacey replied, quickly regaining her composure.

"By the look of her, she doesn't eat at all." Jay said into Luci's ear.

The tour guide continued. "It was obvious to the Franks that any city that could afford to feed grain to pigs was in no danger of starving. A trumpet sounded for a meeting between the two leaders. A cry went up— *"Carcas sonne!"*—and negotiations were made. Charlemagne, out of his great admiration for the Lady Carcas, betrothed her to his trusted adviser, Trencavel, and bestowed the city on them as a wedding present."

Luci nodded. "It takes a woman's touch to conduct a siege properly."

"That's true," Glin replied, looking directly at Luci.

The tour guide smiled. "Yes, but the legend isn't."

"Too bad, it's a good story," Tim commented as he began snapping a series of photos of the entrance to the citadel.

"The reality is far more mundane. The original name of the settlement was Carcaso, which meant fort.

The Trencavel family, as prominent as they were, came much later in the history of the city.

"The fortifications remaining are from the time of King Pedro of Aragon. These made the city impregnable well into the fifteenth century, earning Carcassonne the nickname the Maid of Languedoc."

Fran caught Aimee's eye and pointed to her ears. Aimee removed the headphones and put the cassette player in her backpack.

Luci leaned toward Jay. "I've gotta hear that music! It must be fantastic for her to listen to it twenty-four hours a day!"

"It's all tonalities."

"How do you know?"

"Something Glin said."

Hearing his name, Glin stepped closer to Luci. "It has to do with the manipulation of radio frequencies. It was a Russian inwention." Glin mimicked Mr. Chekov, the navigator from *Star Trek*.

"You guys are kidding me, right?"

Glin shook his head.

Fran gave them a look and they turned their attention back to the tour guide.

"The modern restoration was begun in 1844 by the architect Viollet-le-Duc and is remarkably faithful to the buildings of 1355. The originals were far less dramatic, however, and unfortunately, Viollet-le-Duc was not aware that the southerners used flat roof tiles. What we see now is slate, which was only used in the north. The restoration was completed in 1910.

"The ramparts are composed of fifty-two towers.

The two walls, one inner, one outer, are among the longest fortifications in all of Europe.

"We will now enter la Cité." The tour guide turned and the group walked across the drawbridge.

"I thought there was supposed to be water in moats," Daria said, looking over the edge.

"Who cares? The real issue is how much walking are we going to do?" Stacey replied.

Fran regarded Stacey with great patience. "Walking shoes, Stacey, were on the list."

Stacey glanced down at her expensive flats. "I thought it meant hiking boots with the heavy treads that look like they belong in a monster-truck rally. They would throw any outfit entirely out of balance."

"At the next store, you could get a pair of sneakers," Tim suggested.

Stacey rolled her eyes. "You mean like those dopey little canvas jobbies? I'm so sure."

They continued past the Porte Narbonnaise with the tourist office and arts museum, deciding if they still had any energy, they'd visit them on the way out, along with the souvenir shops.

"It's the same everyplace," Jay muttered as they strolled down Rue Cros Mayrevieille. "Tourist gew-gaws."

Luci stopped at the *boulangerie* window and studied the rounded loaves of crusty bread, studded with black olives. "You're thinking of your father?"

"He's probably selling the same stuff. And those tourists swarming off the love boat are buying them!"

Fran came up behind them. "We can pick up some

things here for lunch if it suits everyone. It's called self-catering."

"That'd be wonderful. I'd like to try one of everything," Luci admitted. Real French bread was likely to be very different from anything available in America.

"And you should," Fran replied. "You can learn a great deal about a culture by what they eat. I always try to encourage the kids to sample as many things as they're comfortable with. Sometimes it works out. Sometimes it doesn't."

"Like if someone has a food phobia," Jay said.

"Right. Some people don't like fish. Some people won't try goat."

Stacey walked by.

"And some people won't eat butter," Jay added.

"Would it be possible to stop at a supermarket?" Luci asked. "I'd feel the trip wasn't complete if I didn't."

Fran raised her eyebrows. "I've never had anyone request that particular destination before, but I have no objection. The first Monoprix we see is all yours."

Fran walked on ahead as Jay and Luci ambled slowly along behind the rest of the group.

They continued on to the center of the Cité, the Place du Château, and crossed another moat to take the tour of the Château Comtal, which included the twelfth-century castle and the ramparts.

As they stood high above the city the guide paused. "You may have heard of the siege of Carcassonne. The Crusaders took the city with odds of fifteen to one. Still, there are those who think the inhabitants would have successfully defended the city if it had not been for the August drought. All twenty-two of the city's wells ran dry and many people became gravely ill.

"The Crusaders were led by Simon de Montfort, and while he is buried here, he was killed by a stone launched from a mangonel at the siege of Toulouse in 1218."

"What's a mang—whatever it was?" Daria asked.

"A mangonel is like a catapult," Glin explained. "It had a swing arm. The device was cocked, loaded, and then released. Simple but very effective."

"I wouldn't expect the aim to be reliable," Logan commented.

"I would suspect that after a number of tries, you'd get a pretty good idea where the rock would land," Glin replied.

Logan still looked dubious. "Good luck would have to play a big role in hitting as small a target as Simon de Montfort," he said.

The guide continued with the lecture. "The war began with an army of thirty thousand knights descending upon the Languedoc, and lasted almost forty years. It ended with the siege of Montsegur in 1244."

"That was the Cathar stronghold?" Jay asked.

"Yes, it was. Some have said the fortress looks like a celestial ark poised high above the valley," the guide went on. "As with any dramatic event in history, legends arise. It's said that the Cathars had a treasure with them at Montsegur but it was removed just before the fall and hasn't been seen since."

"What kind of treasure?" Logan asked.

The tour guide laughed lightly. "It's been said to

have been many things. Gold. Jewels. Secrets. The Holy Grail."

About an hour later Luci and Jay were settling themselves on a grassy area, tearing into fresh bread and cheese. "I've been curious," Luci started. "Last night you said it was a problem that Logan might be interested in you. Why?"

Jay opened the top of her mineral-water bottle and took a sip. "It's complicated."

"Is there someone else?"

"No. Yes. Ehh!" Jay shook her head.

"So you just be friendly. A week from now and you'll never see him again, right?"

Jay nodded and chewed a piece of bread. "It's not so much Logan. It reminds me of the situation."

Luci paused for a moment. "Am I prying?"

Jay quickly reached out and touched Luci's arm. "No, it's not that. I meant it when I said we should be able to say anything to each other. If you're going to be best friends with someone, then there should be no secrets."

"You think we're going to be best friends?"

"Yes. Don't you?"

"I was hoping."

Jay held out a piece of Brie to Luci. "There is someone back in Montreal. . . ."

Luci took the cheese, soft and bulging in its silky rind.

"Is there room for us here?" Logan asked as he sat down between them, followed by Glin, who positioned himself next to Luci, forming a circle.

Luci nodded and busied herself with her bottle of water.

"What about this treasure?" Logan asked.

"Right. This was all very interesting," Jay began. "But we don't know much more about the Cathars than when we arrived. Are we going on to that other place? Mont . . ."

". . . segur," Glin supplied.

"We can't be in the neighborhood and not check this out," Logan stated.

"It's not on the itinerary," Luci reminded him.

"What are you trying to say?" Logan challenged her.

Luci wasn't shaken a bit. "I'm not trying to say anything. What I am saying is we really have to ask Stacey first."

They glanced to Stacey, who had her shoes off and was rubbing her feet as though she was in tremendous pain.

No one said anything for a while.

"Who's going to ask her?"

Jay looked at Logan.

Luci nodded. "Yeah. Perfect."

Logan glanced up. "What? Why me?"

"Duh," Glin replied.

Logan shook his head.

"She likes you," Glin said.

"What makes you think that?" Logan asked.

"For one thing, the way she fell all over you on the plane," Jay said.

"She lost her balance. There was some turbulence."

Luci didn't buy it. "I didn't feel any turbulence."

"Neither did I," Jay agreed.

"Go sweet-talk her. She won't say no to you."

Logan looked back at Stacey. Fran was handing her a Band-Aid. "Guys . . ."

They said nothing.

"We'll still outvote her. We'll always have four even if Aimee goes to their side," Logan said. "That's a girl who's several nuts short of a Crunch bar."

"How can you tell?" Luci asked. "Aimee hasn't said anything for two days."

"Let's not judge her until she becomes verbal," Glin suggested.

Logan spread a thick layer of cheese on some bread. "Okay, okay. I'll ask. After lunch." He took a large bite of his sandwich.

Daria arrived with Stacey, who hobbled over and gently squeezed herself in between Jay and Logan. She glanced at Jay's plate. "Are you girls eating *cheese*? With all that fat in it? I haven't eaten cheese in years."

Luci looked at the food in front of them. There was a wedge of buttery St. André, blue-veined Roquefort, nutty Mimolette, sweet Doux de Montagne, and Brebignal made in the Pyrenees from sheep's milk. Bread, croissants, three kinds of tarts.

It was true Luci's mother was well rounded. And the fact was that so was Luci's father. It could be easily said that Luci wasn't giving Kate Moss a run for her thin money. She knew she'd never be as tall and elegant as Jay, and so what? It was okay to be just the way she was. She cut herself a wedge of St. André and balanced it on a slice of apple all the way to her mouth.

"What's that?" Glin asked, pointing to a wedge of cheese.

Luci picked up a knife and cut him a piece. "Gapéron. It's flavored with garlic. It goes beautifully with the olive bread."

Glin took the bread and cheese from her and took a bite. "That *is* good. We have a lot of cheddar in Vermont but not much else. Still the Green Mountains are pretty. Have you ever been there?"

"Once. Long ago," Luci replied.

"Maybe you can come up when the leaves are turning. You can be a leaf peeker," Glin suggested.

Daria appeared confused. "A what?"

"A tourist that comes to Vermont in the fall just to see the leaves turn color is called a leaf peeker."

"Are you serious? People do that?" Daria asked.

Glin nodded.

"Well . . ." Stacey said. "There's really no accounting for taste, is there?"

"No, there isn't." Jay took a bite of apple and looked at Logan.

"Stacey," Logan began.

"Yes?" Stacey smiled at him.

"We . . . uh, we'd like to go to another town, it's called Montsegur."

Stacey's smile faded. "What's there?"

"A shell of a fortress," Glin replied.

"And stairs," Luci added.

"Lots of stairs," Jay said.

"No. Absolutely not," Stacey answered firmly.

Chapter Six

"**I don't want to walk up another set of** stairs in my life!" Stacey wailed as they reached the top of the fortress of Montsegur.

They were 1,207 meters up a rocky cliff called the Pog (*Pueg* in Occitan for mountain) and the green valley stretched before them for miles. It would have been the perfect secluded location for people hiding from the outside world.

"You could hang-glide from up here," Logan commented as he looked over the edge, breaking the ethereal feeling of being skyborne.

"No thanks," Luci replied. "I prefer both feet on the ground."

"I can just imagine jumping off this wall," Jay said. "If you knew my luck with crashing kites, you'd know why I'd pass."

"A kite is an airfoil just like an airplane wing or a sail," Logan explained.

Jay nodded politely. Stacey stepped closer to Logan, her back to Jay. "Does a kite create a vacuum the way an airplane wing does?"

Logan regarded her with surprise and some admiration.

Jay turned and looped her arm around Luci's, propelling her to the other edge of the tower. "Competitor Stacey Rush—going for her second attempt."

"Maybe he'll get interested in her."

Fran came up behind them. "Discussing history?"

"Umm . . ."

Fran nodded. "Talking about Stacey, huh?"

"Well, Fran. She is obvious," Luci remarked.

Fran ran her fingers through her hair, but the breeze just tousled it again. "We all have our approaches. Maybe that's what works in her world."

"Could be," Jay said. "What is her world?"

"Her father's in show business. Television, I think." Fran was about to turn, then stopped. "You wanted to experience the world, so you're traveling. Part of understanding the world is getting to know the differences in people wherever they're from. Just because Stacey lives in Santa Monica and not Sri Lanka shouldn't give you the impression that you can't learn something from her."

Fran gave them both reassuring pats and returned to Tim, who was engrossed in taking a photo of a lichen-covered stone.

It was true. Maybe Stacey had some exciting stories to tell. Maybe she knew someone famous. Maybe her father was someone famous.

"Have you ever heard of anyone famous named Rush?"

Jay thought for a moment. "No."

"Me neither."

Luci's eye was caught by Glin standing at the far end of the fortress. His long hair was blowing back in the breeze. Sometimes he tied it back with a thin piece of leather with a few ceramic beads on the ends. Today he was wearing a faded light green polo shirt not tucked into his jeans. There was nothing unusual about the way he was dressed, but he looked fantastic.

"If you keep looking at him, he'll notice," Jay told her.

Luci shook herself. "I was looking at . . . at that mountain."

"Uh-huh. Go over and talk to him."

"I couldn't do that."

"Why not?"

"I fell flat on my face at the airport. He probably thinks I'm the biggest klutz he's ever met."

"That was an icebreaker. Stacey would have paid good money to have gotten Logan's attention that way!"

Luci had to laugh along with Jay, but she knew the truth. "I wouldn't know what to say."

Idly, Jay twisted her hair into a knot, shoved the end in, and to Luci's amazement, it stayed on top of her head. "You'll think of something. Trust me."

Luci trusted Jay. She just wasn't so sure about herself.

Fran waved to them. A large enough group had gathered and the tour guide was beginning her talk.

"*Bonjour*. Welcome to Montsegur, one of the centers of the Cathar religion in the thirteenth century. This fortress, build by Guillaume 'Short Nose,' the Duke of Aquitaine, became the symbol of resistance for the nobles of Languedoc who valiantly attempted to defend their land from the invading Crusaders."

"Are there still Cathars today?" an older woman asked the guide.

She smiled. "No, the Cathar religion was effectively terminated in 1244. People today do embrace some of the same beliefs and often come here to acknowledge certain shared ideas and feelings."

"What did the Cathars believe?" Jay asked.

"Even though it is seven hundred years ago, we have quite detailed records."

The group followed her along the wall of the fortress.

"The Cathars believed in reincarnation," Aimee said.

Everyone on the tour faced Aimee, mouths open in stunned surprise.

"Yes," the guide replied, pleased. "That is true."

Aimee pulled back the headphones and let them rest on her neck. "They believed everyone could know God through their own experience rather than through a church or a priest," she continued. "The church didn't like this freedom of thought and worship. Still, no matter how hard they tried to surpress those they called heretics, they never managed to eradicate those individuals who insisted on thinking for themselves."

Jay leaned over to Luci. "Can you believe it? The

first time she speaks and it's like a college lecture on comparative religion."

They continued around the fortress, sparse, rocky, and small. How all those people managed to resist a siege for as long as they had, in such cramped quarters, was nothing short of a miracle.

Jay fell into step next to Aimee. "I was so impressed with what you know. How did you learn all of that?"

Aimee smiled. "Oh, my mother's crazy."

Luci must have looked startled.

"Not in a bad way. Not even in a medical sense. She's a metaphysician."

"Excuse me?" Jay replied.

"A psychic. She studies these things." Aimee pulled the headphones back on.

Luci raised her hands and shrugged in response to Jay's expression.

The tour guide stopped at a window cut into the stone. "The Cathars called themselves Good People. They were quite strict by modern terms, believing that the material world was a far less spiritual place than the next. They cared nothing for possessions or status."

"Then what kind of treasure could they have had?" Logan asked bluntly.

The guide laughed. "The lost treasure of the Cathars. There is quite a legend about that. Languedoc was a wealthy region, conducting lucrative trade with the Mediterranean world. Landholdings were extensive. While most people in the area worshiped in the Cathar way, they were not what is known as *parfaits*—perfects—until they took the *consolamen-*

tum." The guide began walking again. "Usually that was on their deathbed, since it required the renouncing of most earthly pleasures."

"The best ones," Tim commented.

Luci took a glance out the window and blanched. They were perched on the edge of the mountain.

"Are you okay?" Jay asked, catching up with her.

"Yeah, why?"

"You look like you're not having a good time."

"There are two things I don't like. Close spaces and high places. Other than that I'm fine."

Jay laughed. "As long as you stay firmly on the ground in the open, you have no problems."

"Right. Is that too much to ask?"

"No. Stay close to me," Jay told her. "I don't think the tour will last much longer."

The guide began to pick her way carefully down the very steep and ancient steps. "The Cathars were very prosperous, but I have always believed that the treasure was composed of objects they considered sacred, not expensive."

Luci took a deep breath and vowed she wouldn't look down into the valley. She tested the first step. It seemed solid. How long had it been since these stairs had been maintained? Could it possibly be since Guillaume built the place?

"If the fortress was surrounded, how was the treasure removed?" Logan asked.

Everyone stopped as the guide paused to answer him, and Luci wanted to stuff her guidebook in his mouth. Ask questions on the ground!

"Montsegur had been under siege for ten months,

and it was obvious to everyone that the fall was near. Ten thousand men waited at the base of the Pog, but this is a large mountain and there were breaks in the blockade. There were soldiers who were sympathetic to the Cathar doctrine as well. In January of 1244, two *parfaits* are said to have removed what gold was stored here and brought it to a cave. There are many in this region."

"People must have searched for this treasure," Logan said.

"Yes. The legend also says this wealth was later removed to another location."

Okay, fine. No more questions, Luci thought. Let's go.

The tour guide continued speaking. "Whatever wealth the Cathars possessed, it's never been seen since."

They began walking again and Luci put her hand on the wall to keep as far from the edge as possible.

"Three months later the remaining Cathars yielded under surprisingly lenient terms," the woman said. "They would receive full pardons if they confessed their sins. The Cathars asked for a two-week truce."

"Was there a reason for that?" Tim asked.

"We don't know why. Perhaps there was a religious ceremony they wanted to conduct. March fourteenth seems to have been a significant date for them. Whatever it was, everyone in the fortress received the *consolamentum,* including some of the hired mercenaries.

"And here's where the mystery begins. The truce expired on March fifteenth. Everyone could have left unharmed if they simply confessed. However, they didn't. On the night of March sixteenth, two *parfaits* rappelled down the sheer side of the mountain, the Col de la Peyre, and escaped with something."

"That's twelve hundred meters," Jay said. "In the dark."

Stacey shook her head firmly. "Nothing could get me to do that."

"They must have believed it was worth risking their lives for," Glin commented.

"Absolutely. The next day everyone left the fortress and all went to their death, standing firm in their faith."

"What kind of treasure could it have been?" Logan wondered. "They couldn't have carried much on their backs."

"That question remains unanswered," the guide told him.

"There's always an answer," Logan replied.

"Perhaps. It's still one of history's mysteries," the guide concluded, and thanked the entire group for visiting, leaving them outside in the sunlight.

"So we've heard the entire Cathar story. Can we go to Saint-Tropez now?" Stacey asked.

This was like watching a movie and having to leave the theater during the last fifteen minutes. Luci wanted to know what happened to the treasure. She wanted to feel that the Cathars had somehow triumphed over their persecutors.

Fran gathered them in a small circle around her. "All right, ladies and gentlemen. Here are the plans as they stand for this evening. I've made reservations at a small hotel in Les Thermes. It's an unspoiled village which reflects life in France as it's been lived for hundreds of years."

Stacey grimaced. "Does that mean we're going to chase geese around with a stick?"

"No," Fran told her. "We can spend the rest of the afternoon taking a bicycle trip."

"I thought we were heading to the Mediterranean," Daria said.

Fran picked her rucksack up off the ground and removed a map. She unfolded it on a large stone and pointed out where they were and where they could stay. The group crowded around to get a better view.

"We wouldn't make it to the coast by tonight anyway," Tim explained. "I spoke to my editor this morning and she asked if I could get some shots of the hot springs in this area. We thought some of you might find that appealing."

"You mean like a spa?" Stacey asked, interest growing.

"This area is famous for its mineral waters. The hotel has a hot spring. The concierge said something about *thermalisme,*" Fran replied.

"What's that?" Logan asked.

"Water treatments, mud baths, mineral purification," Stacey answered, positively glowing. "There's a very exclusive spa near Palm Springs which offers those services, but this would be . . ."

"European," Fran supplied.

"Of course. How long will we be staying there?" Stacey asked.

Chapter Seven

The Getaway Tour van drove alongside the Aude River. The landscape was both green and rocky. There were vineyards and ruined castles, olive groves and small villages. Robert Louis Stevenson had hiked through the region with his donkey, Modestine, in 1878.

Luci didn't even need to turn her head to look at Glin at the end of the bench seat. She could feel him there.

Maybe she should take Jay's advice and just try to talk to him, but the time never seemed to be right. And she still didn't know what to say.

And how could she be more personal?

How would Stacey do it? Drop her bicycle on him?

Barring a traffic accident, what could she say? Something like "Oh, excuse me, Glin. I think you're really magnificent. I love your hair and your gray eyes and the way you hold your guidebook."

Major duh.

If he didn't think she was the biggest klutz in the world after falling out of the plane, he would surely think her socially dysfunctional.

Maybe her mother would have the answer.

"How do you make a call to the States?" Luci asked. "Do you just direct dial?"

Tim glanced in the rearview mirror. "That's all it takes."

Daria turned in her seat in front of Luci. "If you use a public phone, you have to use these." She passed Luci a handful of plastic cards.

"What are they?" Luci asked, turning the colorful cards over in her hands.

"Télécartes. You buy them at the post office and a couple other places."

"They're collectibles," Fran explained. "Something like stamps. Commemorative issues are offered for sale and are prized by collectors."

Luci gave a few of the cards to Jay. "How do they work?"

"It's like a credit card. Each telecarte is worth 120 units, about a hundred francs. You insert it into the phone, and as you speak, money is subtracted until all the credits are used."

"Which is fun in the middle of a call," Stacey commented.

"You can't use actual money?" Jay asked.

"Not anymore," Tim replied.

"So you have to carry a bunch of these things with you at all times? What a bother," Jay commented, and handed the cards to Glin for inspection.

"How do you know when a card is used up?" Jay asked.

"There's a readout on the phone which flashes zero." Daria offered them a few cards wrapped in plastic. "These are still good."

Glin passed the cards forward to Logan. "Is this the wave of the future? One of these for the phone. A different one for the market. Another for the gas station."

Logan gave the cards a cursory glance then handed them back to Daria. "Not a chance. We'll work with a debit card which will be accepted everywhere. One card for everything."

"I like money," Jay said.

"I don't," Stacey said. "It's dirty. You never know where it's been. These are nice and clean. Fresh. The Europeans are so far advanced in matters of health and beauty."

Luci sighed as Stacey began to talk about an exclusive Swiss clinic that offered clients a special diet regimen of herbs guaranteed to encourage the body to operate at peak levels.

After about five minutes Jay had had enough. "So, Stacey, tell us about living in California."

Luci nudged Jay in the side and gave her a questioning look. Why encourage Stacey to talk at even greater length?

"What do you want to know?"

"How far do you live from the beach?"

"We live on the ocean. On the PCH."

PCH, Jay mouthed silently.

Luci shrugged. She didn't know either.

"Pacific Coast Highway," Daria supplied.

"It's as far as my father can get from the studio and still make it in. The traffic is terrible in L.A."

"What kind of studio?" Logan asked.

"He's the executive producer of *All Our Days,* the number-one rated daytime serial."

"A soap," Luci said.

"No one in the business calls them that. Daytime is big time."

Logan was unimpressed. "Uh-huh."

"You know, Alec Baldwin started his acting career in daytime," Stacey continued.

Jay shrugged at Luci.

"Today, if someone was going to transport a fortune, it would be in diamonds. Small and portable," Logan mused.

"What?" Daria asked.

Jay groaned. "The Cathar Treasure again."

"One-track mind," Luci commented.

"It could have been in gold," Glin replied.

"So did Kathleen Turner," Stacey persisted, even though no one was paying any attention. "Marisa Tomei. Christian Slater. Kevin Bacon. Meg Ryan."

Logan shook his head. "Maybe that first effort to remove the Cathar wealth was gold, but the second trip—"

"It didn't have to be more wealth. It could have been something the people prized. Something invaluable," Jay asserted.

"What's more valuable than diamonds and gold?" Stacey asked reasonably.

"Something that represented their faith," Luci told her.

"What would that be?" Daria asked.

"The Holy Grail," Glin said.

"Or it could have been a big, jeweled bucket. They could have called it the Holy Pail," Tim offered, deadpan.

"Tim!" Fran laughed and gave him a tweak on the arm.

Logan was beyond humor. "But if the Cathars cared nothing for material possessions and believed the physical world was nothing compared to the spiritual realm, would it have been a thing?"

"It could have been something simple." Jay said.

"Like?" Logan asked.

"What's a footprint worth?" Jay responded.

"Nothing," Logan replied.

"Right. What's a dinosaur footprint worth?"

Luci smiled. "You can't put a price on it."

"So it could have been the equivalent of someone's footprint," Glin concluded.

"Maybe," Luci granted. "Fran, you followed the route of the pilgrims to Santiago de Compostella. What did people in the Middle Ages put in shrines?"

"Lots of things," Fran said. "A piece of the Virgin Mary's veil. A sliver of the True Cross. And sometimes things we don't understand. One shrine held the skull of Saint John at age twelve," Fran told them.

"Ugh." Daria grimaced.

Luci paused. "How old was Saint John when he died?"

Fran laughed. "An adult."

"That doesn't make sense," Jay protested.

"Exactly. But they believed it. So what the Cathars prized may well have been something we'd consider quite silly," Fran replied.

Luci stared out the window at the passing scenery. Whatever it was, she was sure she wouldn't consider it silly.

The village of Les Thermes was small. The streets were narrow and not one of them seemed to be straight. One boulevard skirted around a very large tree. On the way in, a boy driving a herd of goats held up traffic and no one seemed to mind. At a sidewalk café, people were drinking coffee. It all seemed very French.

They settled into their rooms quickly. Aimee opted for spending the afternoon reading on the terrace. Stacey and Daria decided to use the spa facilities. Fran and Tim tossed a coin to see who would stay with them, and Tim grinned.

"It does give new meaning to the phrase 'go soak your head,'" Tim told Fran as he gave her a quick kiss and ushered the rest of the group into a courtyard where there were bicycles for everyone.

Moments later, Luci, Jay, Glin, and Logan were biking along with Tim up and down the hilly streets, pausing at interesting buildings to notice the architecture, or to see a cat sitting in a window. Tim found a garden where someone's laundry was drying in a gentle breeze and took a photo of the clothesline. The scent of lavender was in the air.

The homes were older and more rustic than any-

thing Luci had seen before, but many of them sported
television antennas on their roofs. French automobiles
were quite small and hurtled down the streets in a great
rush. Tim told the group that gasoline, called *essence*
or *carburant,* cost almost four dollars a gallon, so
people were conservative about their driving. Many
people traveled by bicycle.

Jay pulled her bike to a halt in front of an antique
shop. The window was full of delicate pieces of china
and gently curving chairs. She and Luci studied the
items as the guys went across the street to see what the
café had to offer.

"Come on, we'll have something to drink," Tim
called, and waved them over.

Jay and Luci parked their bicycles alongside the
others and sat down in the shade.

Seeing window planters overflowing with flowers,
Tim excused himself to make a quick trip farther up
the street to take some photos.

They all scrutinized the menus. "I'm not having
soda. That's too expensive," Jay commented.

Luci nodded. "You get a miniature bottle and it
costs a fortune."

The *serveur* came to take the order. *"Bonjour."*

"Bonjour. Un sirop de cassis," Jay told him.

"Avec des glaçons?" he asked.

"S'il vous plait," Jay responded handing him the
menu. *"Merci."*

"Me, too," Luci replied.

"Sure," Glin added.

"Why not?" Logan said.

The man made a notation on his pad and departed.

"What'd we order?" Logan asked.

"Oh." Jay smiled. "Sorry. It's blackberry syrup and soda water with ice. There are other flavors—lemon, mint, and grenadine. That's pomegranate."

"I'm glad we didn't order that," Logan commented.

Luci studied her fingernails for a long moment, wondering how to keep a conversation going on the relative merits of various soda flavors.

She couldn't think of a thing to say. Jay was no help, having leaned back in her chair and closed her eyes to the heat of the day.

The *serveur* returned with the drinks and Luci gratefully took a swallow, happy to have something to do.

"I can't believe that's the end of the mystery," Logan said.

Luci looked at him in confusion.

Jay tapped her arm. "Treasure again."

"Oh."

"There are lots of things that have never been solved," Glin pointed out. "This is one of them. If we had time to stick around, maybe we could track the story down further."

"Something like that doesn't just disappear. If there was a sizable fortune, someone knew where it was hidden."

"What if everyone who knew was killed?" Jay asked.

"People do die with their secrets," Luci said. "If there was a map, it could have been lost."

"Maybe so," Logan said, then drained the rest of his drink. "Where's Tim?"

They glanced up and down the street but didn't see him.

"I guess we wait here," Glin said.

"Remember that market about a block away? I'd really love to go back and have a look around," Luci said.

Logan stood up. "Couldn't hurt. We'll all go."

They paid the bill, got on their bicycles, and pedaled up the street.

The market was small but filled with beautiful fruits and végetables. Everything was colorful and fresh. Luci and Jay walked around the bins, studying everything.

Luci picked up a basket of strawberries and raised them to her nose. "These smell wonderful," she told Jay, and held them out for her to enjoy.

At that moment the shopkeeper descended upon them spewing a torrent of French.

Startled, Luci put down the berries. The shopkeeper seemed to be quite annoyed and didn't stop lecturing even though Luci didn't have a clue as to what he was saying.

"Pardon. Pardon," Jay told him. The man huffed and turned his back on them.

"What was that all about?" Glin asked.

"It seems that you don't touch anything in these markets. You just committed a big American-style sin," Jay explained.

"C'est vrai," an old gentleman said, smiling.

The group turned to him.

"Different ways," he said in heavily accented English. "But not bad."

"Should I buy the strawberries? Would that make him feel better?" Luci asked, concerned.

"*Non,* Monsieur Roche is very irritable. He does not know how to be friendly to anyone."

Monsieur Roche stood in his doorway for a moment. The old gentleman said something to him in French that settled the shopkeeper and he went inside.

The old gentleman proceeded down the street a bit and sat on a nearby bench. He had a noticeable limp and carried a cane. "My name is Georges Denarnaud."

The group introduced themselves in turn.

"Tell me," Georges said. "What are you doing here in Les Thermes?"

"We're Americans on a tour," Luci replied.

"*Bien.* Good. I, too, liked to travel when I was young. What have you seen?"

"Toulouse," Glin said.

"Carcassonne," Jay added.

Logan stepped closer to the bench. "And Montsegur."

"Ah, yes. So you've seen the fortress," Georges said.

"We heard about the lost treasure."

Luci was not surprised that this subject was still at the forefront of Logan's thoughts.

"And have you been to Rennes-le-Château?"

"I've never heard of it," Luci admitted.

Georges smiled. "If you have time, you must go. It's fascinating. A mystery."

"Another mystery," Jay said, groaning.

"What kind of mystery?" Logan asked, hot on the trail of more details.

"Many years ago, during the last century, there was a curé named Bérenger Saunière. My great-aunt Marie was his housekeeper. He made very little money as a priest but was content since he was from Montazels, not far from here. There was a great deal of free time for studying and reading, which he loved. He visited his friend, Abbé Boudet, in Rennes-les-Bains. All in all, a pleasant life."

"Sounds pretty tame," Logan observed.

"Yes, yes. Tame, as you say. Until 1896. Then the curé came into money. He spent freely. He built a house, a tower, and completely restored the church. Curious, *non*?"

"Oui . . ." Jay replied cautiously.

"By 1917, Bérenger Saunière had spent several million dollars," Georges said. "We must ask how he acquired such great sums of money."

"The Cathar Treasure! He found it?" Logan's attention was riveted on Georges. "Don't tell me he died with the secret."

Georges smiled mysteriously. "Go to Rennes-le-Château. Visit the church. Walk the Tour Magdala. Then come back to me. I will tell you more then. You will not be sorry, I assure you."

Chapter Eight

They were all in the library of the hotel, a communal room where guests could relax, have a croissant and café au lait in the afternoon, or simply read the newspaper. It was decorated in French country prints and large, comfortable chairs. A lovely bowl of blue and white blossoms were centered on the coffee table, but there were other flower arrangements positioned around the room.

"You're absolutely not serious."

"Sure we are."

"No."

"It'll be fun."

"No, it won't. It'll be a bore. How many old ruins are we going to schlep through?" Stacey demanded.

Jay looked at Luci. "Schlep?"

"It's sort of to drag yourself. Walk a lot but with a burden," Luci explained.

"This isn't a ruin," Glin replied. "It's a church."

"Oh, that's dandy. This wasn't supposed to be a religious pilgrimage!"

Fran held up her hands for a time-out. "Stacey, calm down."

"Why should I? We keep getting outvoted! I was a good sport about going to the top of that very stupid mountain, but I'm not going to some dinky little village to see some idiotic country house built by an insane monk!"

Everyone was silent for a long moment.

Luci began to wonder if Stacey was right and they were taking advantage of her. She didn't care where they went. Chasing after an old mystery was just as much fun as going anywhere else. But if Stacey didn't feel the same way, she could well be upset.

"If Stacey doesn't want to go to Rennes-le-Château, then maybe we shouldn't go," Glin said.

Logan held up a hand. "If Stacey doesn't want to go, *she* shouldn't go. Why should we give up something *we* want to do?"

Daria seemed to be on the verge of tears. "This is too much like being home." Having said this, she left the room.

"Okay, guys." Fran held up a hand. "Let me have some time alone with Stacey."

The girls returned to their room to wait until dinner. Luci sat by the window while Jay splashed water on her face and dragged a brush through her hair.

The phone rang and Luci picked it up. "Hello."

"*Allô*. I have an overseas call for Mademoiselle Hamilton," the operator said.

Luci held out the phone to Jay. "It's for you."

Jay took the receiver. "Hello? Hi, Mom."

Luci gestured toward the door, asking if Jay wanted some privacy. Jay shook her head.

Luci busied herself with the postcards she was writing to her family and friends. They'd been so busy during the day, she hadn't had the energy to write notes. Even though she suspected she'd return home before the postcards would arrive, Luci thought it was important to send something back.

So far they hadn't even had time to go shopping. Before she even left New York, Luci had decided that she would find things that were completely French and not available in America. Even if that was a bar of soap, a bottle of shampoo, or a candy bar. She had been surprised to see Le Snickers and Le Prell at the stores, so finding something thoroughly French was becoming more of a challenge than she had imagined.

Luci sorted through the handful of postcards she had grabbed on the fly at Carcassonne. Even that seemed a long time ago because they were covering so much territory, going all day and most of the evening, seeing so many things.

This trip was certainly no disappointment. Not even Stacey could tarnish this experience. Luci wondered how she could convey that on a postcard and picked up a pen to try.

Jay's face was lit with delight as she spoke to her mother. "It's been great. Everyone is very nice. With the possible exception of one girl." She happily related where they had been and what they had seen so far. Then there was a long pause as she listened to her mother. Suddenly the smile faded from her face. "When? How can I do anything about that?"

Luci glanced toward Jay, concerned.

"No. That's too bad. Uh-huh. I'll see you in a couple days. Love you. Bye." Jay hung up the receiver and sat on the edge of her bed.

"Bad news?"

"Not really."

"I don't want to pry, but I *am* a good listener."

Jay lay back on the bed and stared up at the ceiling. "Remember I told you there was a guy in Montreal?"

"Yeah. I was curious, but I figured you'd tell me more if you wanted to."

"His name's Sam. We went to the same school."

"That really posh exclusive place?"

"Uh-huh. Except Sam isn't on a scholarship. His parents are very wealthy."

"How wealthy is very wealthy? A) Comfortably well off? B) They never have to think about money again? C) Their grandchildren will never have to think about money if the subject should ever come up and it probably won't?"

Jay smiled. "No to all the above. It's D) Their great great grandchildren won't know the meaning of the word."

Luci nodded. "That qualifies as very wealthy."

Jay stood. "Let's go take a walk."

They went downstairs and out onto the narrow side street. The lights in the buildings were just being turned on, but there were few other people around.

Jay began walking away from the center of town. "Sam isn't one of those trust-fund types. He's sweet.

We met two years ago—*eh!*" Jay stopped speaking abruptly.

"What?"

"His parents don't like me," she finished quickly, and picked up her pace.

Luci hustled to keep up with her. "Why not?"

"Why would you think?"

"I don't know," Luci replied honestly. "I'm crazy about you."

"Thanks, but you're not looking at it from their point of view."

"Which is?"

"I'm biracial. We're not financially secure. I'm not good enough for their son."

Luci was dumbfounded. "They said that?"

"They'd never come out and say it. They have too much breeding to have that kind of integrity. It was okay as long as we seemed to be just friends. Then about a year ago he started getting the heat. They began asking questions. Who did you take to the dance? Who was at the track meet? Have you seen that lovely girl Solange? They'd create parties and make sure someone's beautiful daughter would be there, seated next to Sam at the dinner table. They'd get tickets to a concert or play for him, but it was already arranged that some acceptable girl would be going. The excuse was always that she was a friend of the family or a business acquaintance and it would be so helpful if Sam would just go to this event. Escort this one, baby-sit with that one. It didn't take us long to understand they didn't want Sam seeing me."

"I've never heard of anything so awful."

"No. That's not the terrible part. I love Sam with all my heart and I suspect I always will. He loves me."

"Then you don't have anything to worry about."

"Uh-huh."

"Do you?"

"It's not about that. He won't stand up to them. He won't stop seeing me, but he won't tell them what's in his heart."

"You're right. That's worse."

"We've had this discussion a bunch of times and it never gets resolved. So I figured it was just as well that I moved away and he could find out what he wants to do."

"You'd just give up?"

"I don't think of it as giving up. I'm not going to be in a relationship where someone isn't going to commit. Sam has to be able to take a position in his life and hold to it."

Luci sighed. "So what did your mother say?"

"Sam's been looking for me. He wanted to know where I was, how to contact me. I told her not to give him the number here."

"You're braver than I could ever be."

They had made a complete circuit around the block. "Don't count on it," Jay replied as they headed for the hotel's terrace, where they found a seat on a double swing.

They swung gently back and forth for a few minutes as the sky began changing colors.

"You can just stay away from Sam?" Luci asked.

"I can do whatever I have to," Jay replied.

Luci didn't doubt that for a moment.

The back door opened; Glin and Logan stepped out.

"We've been looking for you," Logan said.

Luci felt Jay slump deeper into the seat. "Why?" she asked.

"Don't you think we should talk about Stacey?"

Luci groaned. "Not really."

No one said anything and the sky grew increasingly dark.

"The French call this *l'heure bleue*," Jay remarked.

Luci knew enough French to translate that. The blue hour. How appropriate, she thought dismally.

"Do you really want to leave this area without checking out this mystery?" Logan asked them.

"It's not as important to me as it apparently is to you," Jay replied.

"I don't care where I go, I'm just glad to be here," Luci added.

Glin put his feet up on the garden wall.

Logan looked at him. "Well?"

"Not everyone shares your interests so completely."

"I can't believe you're all so complacent!"

Luci was startled. "What you're reading as complacent is our concern for Stacey," she said, then paused. "I don't want to put words in anyone's mouth, but I think that's what it is. Is that what it is?"

Jay pushed the swing harder. "I'm no fan of Stacey's. I think she's throwing a temper tantrum and I don't think she should be rewarded for bad behavior."

That Jay should feel that way made sense to Luci now. She expected everyone around her to be just as straightforward, reasonable, and determined as she was.

"Okay, then," Logan said.

"But," Jay continued, "I'm not her mother, either. I don't think we should run roughshod over her."

"Let her sit in the mud some more," Logan suggested. "We're here and I want to go to Rennes-le-Château. Maybe the country villa is just another Winchester House where the staircases lead nowhere, but doesn't that tell us as much as another cathedral would?"

Luci tended to agree with Logan on that point.

"There must be something Stacey wants that we could use to barter with her on this."

"Yeah, you," Jay replied.

"Be serious," Logan said.

"That is serious, Logan," Luci affirmed. "Stacey's got a thing for you."

"Geez, Louise," Logan said.

"You didn't notice?" Glin asked.

"You don't think I have anything else on my mind?"

It came as a surprise to Luci that Logan had missed Stacey's obvious attempt to get him to notice her. Everyone else in the plane noticed. Maybe guys could have something else on their minds. Was that really possible?

"She fell into you on the plane! How'd you miss that?" Glin said.

"I thought she lost her balance. The way she . . . walks. Those little shoes!" Logan pointed at Luci. "Why didn't you say something?"

Luci gulped. "Me? I've known you for fifteen

minutes! I'm not butting into your life! For all we know, you wanted her falling on you."

Logan looked at Jay. "You thought I wanted her falling on me?"

"Luci said we didn't know," Jay reiterated firmly.

Logan shook his head. "I can't believe this!"

Glin stood up. "Okay, okay. We can't fight among ourselves."

Luci nodded. "Right. Let's not do that."

"What's the bottom line?" Logan wanted to know.

"Whatever the deal with Stacey is, it can be resolved."

"How?" Jay asked.

"We give her Logan and go to Rennes-le-Château without him," Glin replied.

"What?" Logan shouted.

Glin laughed. "Gotcha! We involve her in the decision-making process. We let her have some input."

"She won't have anything to complain about if she wants to go where we happen to want to go," Luci admitted.

"You could try to charm her a little," Jay suggested.

"I don't think so," Logan said quickly.

Glin put his hand on Logan's shoulder. "We're not telling you to take her to the prom. Just jolly her up a bit."

"I think it would work," Luci said.

Logan sighed. "Fine. I'll do it. . . ."

"Great!" The three answered in unison.

"Under one condition," Logan continued.

Jay wrinkled her nose. "I hate conditions."

"The rest of you have to jolly her up, too. Just so she doesn't get the wrong idea about me."

The others thought about this notion for a moment, then agreed.

They went to a small bistro for dinner and no one mentioned anything about the next stop on their itinerary. Fran and Tim led the conversation, asking the group various questions. Without them, there would have been silence.

Only Aimee seemed cheery. She kept herself apart from the others, listening to her music, reading her books and magazines, and only tuning in to the group when something happened.

Daria was positively glum.

Stacey was maintaining her composure. Luci felt there was a lot of practice behind this facade.

A dog came up to Stacey and put his nose on her leg.

"Get away from me!" Stacey commanded.

The dog remained.

"What is this dog doing here, anyway?"

Fran smiled. "Dogs are allowed in restaurants in France."

"That's unsanitary," Stacey decreed, and pushed the dog away. "What does he want?"

"Maybe he likes that perfume, Décadence." Jay suggested. "It's quite vivid."

"It's supposed to be!" Stacey flapped her napkin in front of the dog's face. He looked up at her for a moment and then walked away.

"Everyone done?" Fran asked.

They all agreed they had eaten their fill and couldn't stuff another bite into their mouths—except Stacey, who had told them she had a policy of always leaving the table a little hungry.

With dinner finished, Fran suggested a walk to the center of town.

Logan was about to beg off.

"It's a big local celebration," Fran told them.

Luci understood what this meant. They were supposed to go whether they wanted to or not. "What are they celebrating?" This wasn't any holiday Luci was familiar with.

"This is the festival commemorating Saint Sulpice," Fran replied.

"Him. The famous saint of . . . babbling brooks?" Tim supplied.

"The patron saint of . . . um, I don't know," Fran admitted.

Up ahead, they could see colored lights and hear music playing.

"Pop quiz. Who's the patron saint of love?" Tim asked.

"Saint Valentine," Stacey replied.

"Love as we know it originated right here in Languedoc about eight hundred years ago," Glin said.

"People didn't fall in love before that?" Stacey seemed genuinely surprised.

"Of course they did, but it wasn't expected and there wasn't a literature devoted to it. Then the troubadours, poets, and bards developed the concept of courtly love. Romantic love. Chivalry. It began a new literary form."

It seemed that most of the townspeople had gathered in the square to feast and celebrate. There was a band playing music and a dance floor where people of all ages were swaying in time to the music.

"What's a bard?" Daria asked.

"A poet: singer. They were often traveling performers, going from town to town, or court to court. Since they composed in the language of this region, Oc, which is pretty obscure, we don't see much of their poetry. But it was very beautiful," Glin explained.

"How do you know so much about the troubadours, Glin?" Tim asked.

"My mother is a professor of medieval studies. She translates Oc."

Sure. His mother didn't make croutons. She was slaving over ancient texts in strangely exotic libraries while Lori McKennitt was sautéing bread cubes.

No wonder Glin didn't seem quite of this world. He undoubtedly had one foot in the past at all times. Luci felt as colorless as a sheet of waxed paper.

"So all that stuff about knights on white horses and ladies in long dresses came from here." Daria said.

"That's more of a Hollywood notion than reality. Yes, knights did dedicate themselves to a certain lady. She was often someone who he couldn't have for one reason or another, so it wasn't always a happy arrangement," Glin replied.

"Don't forget this was a very wealthy area, very cultured. The climate is mild. There was time for romance and art. In other countries where there was more of a struggle to survive, some of these traditions never caught the imagination of the people," Fran added.

"What did they sing about? Is it anything we'd understand?" Daria asked.

"One of the greatest Occitan poets was Arnaut Daniel. He wrote this," Glin said, and began to recite:

"I am blind to others and their retort
I hear not. In her alone, I see . . .
I could not walk roads, flats, dales, hills
   by chance,
To find charm's sum within one single frame
As God set in her. . . ."

As he finished speaking, Glin looked at Luci. It was like taking the first hill on the big roller coaster. Her stomach dropped right to her feet.

She felt Jay at her back. "Don't faint," Jay whispered.

Around her, music was playing and people were going out onto the dance floor. Tim whirled Fran away.

Glin held out his hand to Luci.

Luci willed herself to breathe, then put her hand in his.

Chapter Nine

G lin led Luci out onto the dance floor and pulled her closer. They began swaying with the rhythm of the music.

He smelled something like gingerbread, spicy and comforting, and she could feel the warmth of him next to her. It seemed like they were moving in slow motion, but her head was spinning. Was she dancing or was she in free fall?

Then, all too soon, the music stopped.

Glin released her hand and stepped back. "Thank you for the dance, Luci."

"Thank you."

Thank you? Why did she say that? She should have said you're welcome.

No. That wasn't good either.

She should have said yeah, it was great. Gone for the casual reply as though she'd danced with a lot of guys.

But she hadn't.

Luci had gone to school dances, but she had always avoided slow dances because the whole idea made her uncomfortable. If she slow-danced with a guy who was a friend, it seemed silly. If she slow-danced with a guy she didn't really like, his hand on her back would feel like a dead fish hanging on her. The music could never end too soon.

She had wondered if it could be different. Now she knew the answer. It definitely was different.

They both returned to the group and the music started up again. Glin took Jay's hand. Logan took hers. Tim whirled Stacey in several circles while Fran applauded wholeheartedly.

It was just a tour. They were just having fun. Dancing was part of having fun.

It didn't mean anything.

It could be sitting next to each other at dinner or in the van. It could be playing tennis or sitting on a terrace. Seven days and they'd go their own separate ways.

That was probably a good thing. Any longer and people could get too attached to each other.

That night Luci couldn't sleep. She tossed and turned. The pillow seemed too flat. She tried to plump it up.

She lay on her back. Her side. Her stomach. She sat up in the dark until she couldn't stand it any longer. At home, Luci would have read, but she didn't want to turn on the light in case it disturbed Jay.

As quietly as possible, Luci got out of bed, pulled

on her robe, and left the room. She went downstairs and out onto the terrace.

The night was warm and she settled herself into the swing, pulling her legs up close to her.

It was important to maintain a casual attitude. No matter what she felt, she couldn't start acting like an idiot. Not only would she embarrass herself, she'd embarrass Glin, and she'd never want to do that.

He was simply a very nice guy. No, amend that. He was simply a very attractive, nice guy. No, that wasn't right either. He was a fabulously attractive, nice guy, which was why he asked her to dance.

He probably had a girlfriend back home. How the girls in Vermont could let him get away was beyond logic. He had taken these tours before and undoubtedly got along with all the girls. He probably forgot them afterward just like he'd forgot her.

And she'd forget him.

"Who are you kidding?" Luci asked herself aloud.

"Who are you talking to?" Jay asked.

The sound of another voice made Luci jump. "Yikes! You nearly scared me out of my skin!"

Jay plunked herself down on the swing. "I was worried about you. When I woke up, you weren't there."

"I couldn't sleep."

"Neither could I. Thinking too hard?"

Luci nodded.

"Me, too."

"About Sam?"

Jay nodded. "About Glin?"

"Silly, huh?"

"You or me?"

"Me, of course."

"I wouldn't say that."

"You have a relationship with Sam. I'm just a fellow traveler to Glin. This is strictly one-sided."

"Are you sure about either of those?"

Luci paused for a moment. The swing gently rocked back and forth, sqeaking as it went. "No."

"Me neither."

"Terribilis est locus iste."

"What does that mean?"

"This place is terrible," Luci translated the inscription on the lintel above the entrance. "One semester of Latin is required at my school. I never thought it would come in handy, though."

Stacey stepped through the doorway of the Church of the Magdalen. "I wouldn't say it's terrible, but I have seen better interior decoration."

They had left Les Thermes early that morning to make the trip to Rennes-le-Château. The drive in the van took only a few minutes, passing through the valley and along a surprisingly good road.

They passed a small farm with several cows grazing in a pasture.

"You live on a ranch, don't you, Daria?" Fran asked.

Daria said she did.

Jay perked up. "What's it like?"

"Do you have cattle?" Logan asked.

"Do you have roundups?" Tim asked.

Daria began twisting a lock of hair around her forefinger. "It's not exactly that kind of ranch."

Fran turned slightly in the front seat. "Ranches raise other animals besides cattle. Ostriches, for instance."

"We don't have those. We have four cows."

"So how big is this ranch if you only have four cows?" Logan asked.

"Four hundred acres."

"Wow," Jay exclaimed. "That's a lot of land."

"Not in Peralta. There are ten-thousand-acre ranches right down the road from us."

"So is your father a rancher?" Glin asked.

"No, he's an investment manager. But he's sort of retired now. He gave up the business a couple years ago and we moved to California. Someplace to have a future. Quality lifestyle. No crime."

"Where is Peralta? Is it near Los Angeles?" Jay asked.

Stacey was expertly threading her hair together in a French braid. There were no loose ends, no flyaway strands. "It's up the coast a hundred miles or so."

Daria nodded.

"What makes it a ranch, then?" Jay asked.

"It used to be a working ranch. It was first a camp for the Porter Soup family. People used to winter in the area. Society types."

"It's a very beautiful area," Stacey said. "They've used Peralta for many movies locations."

"Any movies we'd know?" Fran asked.

"*Of Mice and Men*."

Luci shook her head. "I missed that one. I don't go to the movies to be depressed."

"What was so depressing about that?" Stacey asked.

"People were mean to each other," Luci replied.

"It is a classic," Stacey pointed out.

"So is *A Room with a View* and no one was mean in that story."

"Then you'd better stick to the G-rated films," Stacey commented.

"I don't go to the movies very often. You pay all that money and you don't even walk out of the theater with anything in your hand. You can pay nearly the same amount of money for a video and watch it again and again. That's a better deal."

"Luckily for the entertainment industry, you are not the average American."

Instead of taking that as an insult, Luci felt complimented.

Fran clapped her hands. "Okay, tourists. May I have your attention? Rennes-le-Château is directly ahead."

Everyone in the van tried to get the best view possible of the town situated on a little mountaintop dotted with trees and surrounded by farmland.

It was an old settlement. In prehistoric times, the Celts had considered it a sacred site. Romans had found the settlement appealing because of the therapeutic hot springs. The honeycombed caves in the region were used as mines.

Later, in the sixth century, the settlement's population virtually exploded to nearly thirty thousand people. At that time it was the prime residence of the Visigoths, the Teutonic tribe who had overturned the Roman Empire. As the Visigoths lost prominence in the region, the population of the town dwindled until it reached its present modest size.

The tourists stepped into the dark and cool church.

"Yikes," Daria gasped as she nearly bumped into a large gargoylelike statue. "What's that?"

Fran had picked up a small information sheet available in town that described the local attractions. "This rather unpleasant fellow is Asmodeus."

"I'm not familiar with that individual," Luci said.

Fran read a bit further and then studied the statue. "It's not a person. It's a demon."

"Demons in churches?" Logan asked. "I thought the whole point was to get rid of the demons. Get thee behind me, Satan, and all that."

Fran checked the sheet again. "This seems to be a little different approach."

"Since when?" Logan persisted.

"Since the reconstruction instituted by the parish priest, Bérenger Saunière, in the 1890s. The original church was built in 1059, but the foundation derived from a sixth-century Visigoth structure."

"It gives me the chills," Stacey remarked, and walked away.

"It says Asmodeus is the custodian of secrets and the guardian of hidden treasures."

"*Yes!*" Logan nearly shouted.

"Ssshhh!" They all called at him.

"We're on the right trail," he assured them.

They continued through the church, studying the architecture, the decorations, the floor for any clues or inconsistencies. All along the walls were large painted plaques of the Stations of the Cross.

"I don't know," Stacey began. "I have to tell you. This is not my religion, so excuse me if I'm not on the same page as everyone else. Did the baby Jesus come from Scotland?"

"Of course not," Jay replied.

Stacey tilted her head as she stood in front Station Eight. The rest of the group came closer to study the painting.

"So what happened to white? The mother couldn't make up her mind what her favorite color was, so she chose plaid?" Stacey asked.

"This is very weird," Jay said.

"Is that blackwatch tartan that baby's wearing?"

"No, I think it's dress Gordon," Tim said.

Fran shook her head. "Stuart tartan."

Glin approached the plaque. "The baby's wearing a kilt."

Daria pushed closer. "Is not. It's swaddling cloth."

"Okay. Let's cover what we know so far. There's this wigged-out priest and he decides that the Nativity story is getting a little old. It hasn't been revised in two thousand years. He wakes up one morning and decides he wants to bring it into the modern era, and he's got the money from somewhere to do it. So in this version the Three Wise Men show up playing bagpipes. What are they singing?" Luci asked. "Away in the manger *oft gang agley?*"

"To paraphrase Robert Burns," Glin added.

Luci smiled inwardly. Of course he would recognize a line by the Scottish poet. She pictured his family seated at a long library table in front of a crackling fire, all studying far into the long Vermont winter nights. There would be no television at the Woods house to disturb the scholarly atmosphere.

Logan laughed. "The wise men can arrive by train instead of camels, which are so messy."

"It gives a whole new twist to Christmas carols," Jay commented. "Just try blowing 'Jingle Bells' through those squealing pipes."

"Was plaid something used in the Middle East?" Logan asked. "Is this historically correct in any way, shape, or form?"

"Not that I've ever heard," Fran admitted.

"All this is very creepy and I'd rather be outside," Stacey said, and turned to leave. She paused. "I told you that monk wasn't the sharpest knife in the drawer."

Luci strolled around the church. None of it made any sense to her. If the curé had made a hundred dollars a year, even accounting for inflation, he would never have been able to afford the renovation of this church. Where did he get the money?

Maybe Stacey was right and the priest had lost his grip on reality.

But that still didn't explain where he had gotten enough money to become a construction maniac. And it didn't explain why someone thought it was a terrible place.

"Come on, Luci," Jay called to her. "We're going out into the churchyard."

Luci stepped into the sunlight and blinked until her eyes adjusted.

The cemetery had been there for fifteen hundred years. There were remnants from the Visigoths and from every settlement since. The walls were crumbling in some sections; other parts had been patched recently. Next door was the Château d'Hautpoul, also a building that dated back to the sixth century.

Luci's mind swirled with all the history surrounding her. Everything in America was new. A house from the 1900s was old. A saltbox from the 1700s was an antique. Here were buildings easily a thousand years old. It wasn't a museum, set off behind velvet ropes. It was real, in use.

How did those people live? What did they eat? Did they have the same feelings?

Fran was reading her sheet. "This is the sepulcher of Marie, Marquise d'Hautpoul de Blanchefort, who died January seventeenth."

"Those are the people who lived next door," Glin said.

Luci strolled around. "Jay, come here. I found Saunière's grave."

Jay hurried over. "Will you look at that?"

"What?"

"The date. How odd."

"January seventeenth . . . the same date as the neighbor lady."

"That's quite a coincidence."

Aimee smiled. "There are no coincidences."

"The entire history of the town is right here," Fran said.

"Maybe." Logan was paying particular attention to a Visigoth pillar. He pushed at the top.

"Logan, stop that," Fran said.

"I want to see if the top comes off."

"Why would you want to do that?"

"Something could be inside."

Tim whistled. "We are here to look only. Are we ready to go to the tower now?"

"Are we walking?" Stacey asked.

"Yes," Fran replied. "I told you to get sneakers."

"Oh where would I do that? It's not as though we've been within five hundred miles of Galeries Lafayette."

Daria looked confused.

"Big department store," Jay explained.

"Any sneakers would have worked for five days," Tim told her.

Stacey made a face. "A lot you know."

"Shoes are just shoes to me," he admitted.

"See how wrong you are. Shoes are a fashion statement," Stacey declared as she walked on in front of them. "Beyond that, improperly fitting shoes create pressure points which unnecessarily stress your body."

"And properly fitting shoes make" Logan paused, then raised his voice—"happy feet!" He danced a little jig.

The Villa Bethania, Bérenger Saunière's manor, was now owned by a private family, so it wasn't possible to go inside. Tourists were permitted to stroll around the gardens, visit the orangery, and see what remained of the zoological garden.

The villa was a large three-story building made of stone. A large fountain stood in the front yard where fruit trees had once grown. According to the information sheet, Saunière had never taken residence in the house, but Marie had lived there until 1946 when it was sold.

"He goes to all the trouble to build this mansion and

never lives in it," Logan said as they stood in the front yard.

"Maybe it gave him the willies," Stacey remarked. "It's . . ."

"It's got a bad vibration to it," Aimee supplied. She put up her hands, palms facing the building. "Can't you feel it?"

Luci hesitated then put her hands up. She could feel the breeze.

"The only thing I'm starting to feel," Daria said, "is hungry."

Aimee was smiling as she lowered her hands.

"Could you really feel something?" Luci asked her.

"Yes."

"What was it like?"

"If you touch a stereo when it's playing, it has a vibration. That's what I felt."

"How did you know if it was good or bad?" Glin asked.

"Because it's so insistent."

"Is it like a ghost?" Luci asked.

Logan approached. "Could it be Saunière's ghost? Could you communicate with it?"

Jay rolled her eyes.

"Look. I don't believe in ghosts, vibrations, or things that go bump in the night. But it doesn't cost anything to ask." Logan sounded a little defensive.

"What do we do? Have a séance?" Luci asked. "It's probably a good time. The moon's full."

"If that's what it takes, I'd be game," Logan replied.

Aimee turned her cassette player back on. "Whatever's here is much older than the curé, and it doesn't want to talk to you." She pulled the headphones back on.

*   *   *

The Tour Magdala was perched precariously on the edge of a cliff. It had the appearance of a minicastle with crenellations, arches, and narrow windows. The tower was on the corner closest to the sheer drop down the mountainside.

Inside was an incredible library. Many towns would have considered themselves fortunate to have that many volumes. There was beautiful and rare china, sumptuous fabrics, and museum-quality antique marble statues.

"This is unbelievable," Jay said in awe as they surveyed all the curé had collected.

Luci couldn't have agreed more. There was a sizable fortune represented in the tower alone. The information sheet claimed the priest had spent lavishly on his parishioners as well.

"By the look of it, Logan, he spent it all," Luci declared.

Logan shook his head. "I don't think so. If he was still in the process of building when he died, there was something left. He would have allocated enough to last and maybe leave an inheritance to someone else."

"That housekeeper?" Jay asked.

"Yeah, what was her name?"

"Marie. Georges's great-aunt."

"Do you think she got the money?"

"More importantly," Logan put in, "do you think she got the secret of where it came from?"

Glin nodded. "That's something we need to ask Georges, isn't it?"

Chapter Ten

Luci noticed how Logan made a point of sitting next to Stacey on the return ride back to Les Thermes. She also noticed how uncomfortable he seemed to be. Despite that, he got high marks for paying enough attention to ask questions and nod at all the right moments. Luci doubted if she could have held up so well under the onslaught of small talk.

Stacey chatted the entire way. She talked about living in California, about the shopping, about Malibu, which was the ultimate place to live but too far for her father to commute. Her father drove a China-red Mercedes. That wasn't his fun car, which was a mint-condition Jaguar XKE. Stacey longed to drive the Jag, but her father swore she'd never get near it. She was supposed to get a car for her birthday, but it would probably be something like a Mazda RX-7. What she wanted, if she had to have an American car, was a Viper.

Luckily, it wasn't a great distance back to Les Thermes. Luci nearly stumbled out of the van when they arrived. She was certain Stacey had used up all the oxygen in the vehicle and wondered if they were heading to Saint-Tropez, could they pick up some of those little oxygen bottles at a nearby convenience store?

"Is the water in the Mediterranean warmer than the Pacific?" Daria asked.

"It has to be. The Pacific is freezing," Stacey replied.

Jay moved in to Luci. "She should try swimming in Montreal."

They all stood at the front of the hotel for a long minute. Luci felt there was something waiting to be said, but none of them knew how to say it. She knew they had to get back to Georges's cottage, but she had no idea how they were going to arrange that.

The agreement had been to visit Rennes-le-Château. Now that they had, there was no reason for the group to remain in Les Thermes.

"How about some lunch?" Fran suggested.

"I'm up for that," Tim admitted. "All that walking and sightseeing wears me out."

"There's a cute place down the street," Stacey said. "It reminds me of a place on Melrose."

"Uh-huh," Jay replied softly.

At the bistro near the hotel, a white-jacketed *serveur* greeted them.

"*Bonjour, monsieur,*" Fran replied as they were shown to a table in the shade.

Luci was learning that courtesy was very important

to the French. It was expected that customers would greet a *serveur* or shopkeeper appropriately. Luci couldn't imagine doing that in New York City unless she knew the person by name. At the corner deli at rush hour, people stood in line, shoving and shouting at the countermen.

That would never happen in France, Luci was certain. It would have been a horrifying display of bad manners. It would have been . . . well, American.

They studied their menus for a time and discussed the possibilities. Did they want a heavy meal now and just have something light for dinner? That didn't apply to Logan and Glin, who wanted to eat a substantial meal now and another substantial meal later, with a hearty snack in the middle of the afternoon.

"What's steak tartar?" Daria asked.

"I don't think you want that," Luci warned.

"Why not?"

"It's raw beef," Luci replied. "Ground. Hamburger."

Discomforted, Fran placed her menu on the table. "Yeah . . . and it's often . . . um, *cheval*."

Luci looked to Jay.

"Horse," Jay translated.

There were loud groans all around the table.

"You have to be kidding!" Daria exclaimed.

"No, I'm not. This is a different culture."

"Where's Animal Welfare? You can't just go around eating horses," Stacey said emotionally.

"What's the difference between a horse and a cow?" Tim asked.

Luci thought the answer was obvious. "Horses have personalities."

"Actually, without the horse, the history of the world would be entirely different," Glin commented.

Luci gestured with her hand. "See, horses should be respected for that alone!"

"I'm not the one suggesting you . . . should . . . partake. . . . Why don't you all stick to fish?"

"Ick," Daria grimaced.

The *serveur* returned and waited patiently as they still tossed suggestions around the table. Finally, Stacey ordered a salad niçoise with no dressing. The man stared in disbelief. The rest of them chose a bowl of onion soup, topped by bubbling Gruyère cheese. That was followed by a *croque monsieur,* a grilled ham sandwich. It was decided they would walk to the *pâtisserie* for a *religieuse,* a cream puff with a top like a nun's cap.

Luci shook her head as she watched Stacey dig into the large bowl of dry lettuce. She could hardly imagine anything less appealing other than perhaps trying to eat squid.

"Now we're going to Saint-Tropez, right?" Daria asked.

"I have to find at least five more bottles of Décadence," Stacey announced. "And they're certainly not available in this town."

Fran glanced around the table. "That's the plan."

Logan was quick to jump in. "Not today, though. It's too late to start driving now. Isn't it?" He looked at them for confirmation and support.

"Yes. Absolutely," Luci jumped in.

"I think we're probably all pretty tired," Glin added.

"I haven't seen the spa," Jay said.

"You?" Stacey fairly choked on her endive.

"I've heard it's wonderful at night," Jay replied. "The cool night air, the hot water."

Stacey tilted her head back and forth. "I would like another session in the mud bath. It was so purifying."

"Then it's agreed we leave tomorrow morning first thing? And I mean first thing, campers, not eleven o'clock."

Stacey nodded.

"I'm really looking forward to just going right up to the room and conking out," Logan said to no one in particular.

Luci understood. "Me, too. I'm pooped. The moon was shining in my face all night long and I had a lot of trouble sleeping."

Aimee smiled. "The moon's energy is at its peak when it's full. Only someone really attuned to the Lady feels it."

"What lady?" Daria asked.

"The moon is called the Lady," Aimee explained.

Luci always felt she wasn't fully understanding Aimee and probably had missed something important. But there was no way to tell. She had definitely never met anyone like her before.

But then, Luci could easily say that about everyone on the tour.

Logan had more energy than anyone she knew. He was like a bulldog. He got a hold of something and you couldn't pry it out of his mouth.

Jay was rock steady. Completely solid. Luci knew she could always trust Jay's judgment.

Luci looked over to Glin.

Glin. He was the voice of reason. Balance.

He turned toward her in that moment and smiled slightly.

Luci didn't know what to do. She tried to smile a little in return. The fork dropped out of her hand with a clatter and she had to chase it around the table to recapture it.

Stacey watched this. "Do you need a string and a clip like mothers put on mittens so you can hang on to that silverware?"

Luci felt her face grow hot.

No one said anything. They just looked at her.

Luci put the fork down beside her plate carefully then looked Stacey directly in the eye. "If you can spare an extra set, that'd be great. I left my Super Glue at home."

Tim reached for his glass of water and took a quick swig.

Fran bit her lip to keep from laughing.

And Jay patted Luci's leg under the table.

They all returned to their rooms and stayed there for about fifteen minutes. Soon there was a tap on Luci's door. It was Logan, who directed them to meet at the bicycles in five minutes. He went down the hallway and disappeared down the stairs.

Five minutes later, silently, Luci and Jay followed.

The bicycles were waiting and they all got on and coasted down the driveway.

"Do you still have his address?" Logan asked.

Jay held up the piece of paper Georges had given them the day before.

"Do you know where it is?" Luci asked.

"I checked with the concierge," Logan replied.

That figured. Logan would have attended to all the details.

They pedaled quickly to Georges Denarnaud's cottage and leaned the bicycles against the garden wall. Blue morning glories, hollyhocks, dianthus, and portulaca all competed for space in a wild display.

"Do you think he's home?"

"If he's not, we'll wait."

"How much time do you think we'll have before Fran will start wondering where we are?"

"And I have an appointment to look at the mud," Jay said to Luci. "It seems so out of character for Stacey to want to get dirty."

"This is clean dirt," Luci explained.

"Oh."

"I think we've got a couple hours before we're missed," Logan said as they reached the front door. "Around dinner." He knocked firmly.

"If we have to leave tomorrow—" Luci began.

Before she could finish the thought, the door opened.

Georges smiled in delight. "*Bonjour. Bonjour.* You've been to Rennes-le-Château, *non?*"

"Yes."

"*Entrez.* Come in. You want to hear more."

They followed him inside the small cottage and he motioned for them to sit.

It was a simple cottage, and Luci immediately felt comfortable in the room. The walls were white stucco. The furniture was plain but comfortable. There were touches of color throughout the room: a green plant near the window, a painting above the sofa. There was a red-patterned Oriental area rug covering the scrubbed wood floor. A small fireplace took up one wall and was framed by intricate andirons.

Georges lowered himself slowly into a comfortable wing chair. "You know part of the story. The people of town do not speak of the rest, what little more they do know. There are many curiosities which they choose to ignore."

"Like what?" Luci asked. If there were curiosities, she wanted to be able to wonder about them, too.

"After World War Two, the government issued new currency. They wanted to catch profiteers and those who would evade the income tax. It was necessary for everyone to turn in their old money in exchange. I remember my parents doing this. My great-aunt—the curé's housekeeper—did not. She was seen in the garden of Villa Bethania burning large quantities of francs. No explanation, of course."

"Of course," Jay echoed.

"The old woman was eccentric, it was said. She may have been. But where did she get all that money to burn?"

"One more bizarre event connected with this mystery," Logan said.

But Georges wasn't finished. "There is another instance that resists reason. After the priest died, he was positioned in a chair. The villagers filed past and plucked tassels off his cloak as souvenirs."

Luci had never heard of such a ceremony. "Why?"

Georges shrugged. "As I said. A curiosity."

That was an image Luci would ponder for a long

time. Just the notion that anyone would conduct a funeral with the dead person sitting up instead of lying down was ghoulish.

The old gentleman lit a pipe and puffed on it for a moment. "It's said that Marie died with the secret. But that's not true. She confided in me. Marie told me certain things before she died in 1953."

"Not on January seventeenth," Luci said.

Georges laughed. "You noticed that. No, my aunt died on January twenty-ninth. Here is the story as Marie told it to me.

"Being new to his post in Rennes-le-Château, Saunière wanted very much to restore the church, which was falling into great disrepair. He managed to get enough contributions from the villagers to begin the project. As the work progressed, he moved the altar stone. Perhaps you saw it—an old Visigoth pillar?"

"I saw it," Logan said.

"It was hollow."

"See?" Logan interjected.

Georges continued. "Inside, Saunière found ancient documents which have since disappeared. I think they may have found their way to Rome, but I often wonder if they didn't fall into other hands."

"Like who?"

"There were many powerful people in that day and time. Certain royal houses of Europe. Certain ambitious individuals. Certain people with interests out of the ordinary. Who can say now? There is no record."

A puff of smoke drifted toward the ceiling. "Two of the manuscripts were in Latin. They were fairly recent in age and appeared to have been taken from the New

Testament. Saunière assumed they had been placed there by a priest before him. At first, he accepted the texts at face value, but as he studied them further he noticed there was something dreadfully wrong. The words ran together. Some letters were raised, while others were not."

"A code?" Logan asked.

Georges smiled. "You're very bright. Yes, that's what Saunière suspected, so he put himself to the task of deciphering the hidden message."

"Did he succeed?"

"He did. It was then that Saunière realized he had stumbled upon something very important. So important that the Bishop of Carcassonne, upon learning of the message, sent Saunière to Paris, where he remained for three weeks at the seminary of Saint Sulpice."

Luci remembered what Aimee had told them. Nothing is a coincidence. How was it that the town revered the same saint that was connected to the mystery?

"Father Saunière returned to Rennes-le-Château and soon began the building projects which remain to this day. He seemed to have an unlimited source of money."

"From where?"

"People talk. There have been many theories over the years. Rome. The royal houses of Europe. Many famous people visited this area."

"To talk to the priest?"

Georges shrugged. "There is no proof, just a great deal of talk. There are even those who say the good father found an energy source from beyond the stars."

Luci was confused. "You mean something extraterrestrial? From another planet?"

"*Oui. Oui.* How you say? Out of this world. People have great imaginations."

"Maybe the Vatican gave the priest the money to do the reconstruction," Luci suggested. "It could be as simple as that."

"Perhaps. Hitler thought it was more than that."

"Adolf Hitler?"

"Yes. When he came into power in Germany, he, too, heard the stories and the theories. He sent a contingent of German miners into this region to dig through the caves, believing that Saunière had found . . . *le trésor perdu.* . . ."

"The lost treasure," Jay translated.

"*Oui.* The lost treasure of the Cathars . . ."

"Bingo!" Logan exclaimed.

Luci was at the edge of her seat. Jay was twisting her hair into knots. Glin's eyes were bright with excitement.

Georges smiled at their enthusiasm. "I lived here through the war. I saw the miners. I met their leader, Otto Rahn, who had been a scholar before the war. He died under unexplained circumstances not long after he left here."

"Was he murdered?"

Georges shrugged.

"Did he learn something?"

"Monsieur Rahn may have learned something, but the Nazis never found the treasure."

"Had Saunière already found it?"

Georges put down his pipe. "I believe he did, but he

didn't remove it entirely. I have a map. Marie gave it to me shortly before her death. It had been Saunière's. They had often walked the countryside together. Searching. Making the map I possess now." Georges went to a cabinet and removed a parchment. He spread it out on a table and the group gathered around.

Georges lowered himself stiffly into a chair. "For years I searched for the cave designated on this map. Every spare moment I had was spent in the surrounding mountains. It nearly cost me my life." He patted his leg. "This limp I carry with me now is a result of that. Since then, I've been unable to pursue my search. I've waited for many years to find someone I could trust to take my place. I believe I can trust you."

"And you imagine the treasure is still there?" Glin asked.

"Yes. What may remain, I can only guess."

"Is it far from here?" Logan asked.

"*Non*. Not far at all. There are a lifetime of caves to explore in this region. I was fortunate to have come upon this one."

"What do you want from us?" Glin asked.

"I offer you this map. Go to the cave. Seek *le trésor perdu* for yourselves."

"How will we know it's the right cave?" Luci wondered.

"The Cathars always left their mark. How do you say it? A pentagram."

Georges held out the map to them.

Chapter Eleven

Gingerly, Logan took the fragile map into his hands.

"I think you are brave enough to follow the path," Georges said.

Logan nodded.

"Then you will know the truth of Saunière's secret." Georges smiled.

Jay checked her watch. "We'd better get going or Fran will wonder where we are."

"I'll bring the map back," Logan said as they walked to the door.

"*D'accord. Bonne chance.* I'm sure you'll have much to tell me." Georges opened the door and they walked into his garden. "*Au revoir!*"

They went to their bicycles.

"You're losing it," Luci told Logan.

"What do you mean?"

"Taking the map from that man?"

"Yes?"

"We're leaving tomorrow. We don't have time to go spelunking!" Luci said.

They began to pedal away from the cottage. "I think it's called caving."

"I don't care what it's called. We don't have time. So you've taken the map under false pretenses."

"What are you so upset about?" Logan asked. "You came for an adventure and here it is."

"I can picture it now. We'll go to Stacey and tell her how great it will be to go crawling around in a dark old cave instead of going to a boutique on the seashore. I think she'll buy that, what do you think, Jay?"

"I think the old man is out of his mind."

Glin pedaled closer to the group. "He seemed very nice to me."

Jay pedaled harder. "Did I say he wasn't nice? He can be as sweet as maple sugar, doesn't mean he isn't crazy as a loon, too."

"All the more reason we shouldn't listen to him," Luci said.

"Don't then," Logan replied. "I want to go the cave. If you want to go, you're more than welcome. If you don't want to go, don't." He pedaled ahead.

"When do you think you'll have *time* to go?" Luci shouted.

"Tonight," Logan shouted back without turning around.

"He's crazy," Jay said. "Absolutely nuts."

"He's going to go to a cave in the middle of the night? Good luck," Luci commented sourly.

"You have to understand Logan. How he grew up. All this affects how he approaches life," Glin said.

Jay stopped her bicycle at the curb. "Make us understand so this will make sense. But I don't think you can."

Glin propped his bike against a streetlight. "Logan's father was a fighter pilot in the air force. He flies corporate jets now. This is a man who was brought up on a huge ranch in Montana. He won't sleep inside if he can sleep outside. That's how Logan was raised. They go hunting and fishing together. Snowshoeing."

"Where's his mother?"

"She couldn't take it. Literally. She wanted to sleep inside, have a house with windows and screens. From what Logan's told me, she's a wonderful woman, but she's not a mountain man."

Jay grimaced. "Mr. Carlisle's one of those macho men?"

Glin shook his head. "I wouldn't say that at all. He's very kind, has a great sense of humor, would do anything in the world for Logan or one of his friends. He's just not . . ."

"Housebroken?" Luci supplied.

"Something like that. That's the only way Logan knows the world. A very physical approach. A survivalist."

"That's ducky, but what's it all got to do with this?"

"Logan sees this as an adventure, as a test. What would he say to his father if he had the opportunity to search for the treasure and chose to sleep in bed instead?"

"Then he should come back with his father," Luci reasoned.

Glin took a hold of his bike. "You only go through life once. I don't want to miss this either."

"The only time to go would be tonight," Jay observed.

Glin got on the bike. "Then we go tonight." He began pedaling away.

Luci sat on the curb. "This is really frustrating."

"Why?" Jay asked as she sat down next to her.

"I want the adventure, too."

"But?"

"There were no specific rules that we shouldn't leave the hotel at night, but you know that's what they mean. We'd be so finished with this tour they wouldn't let us read the newspaper advertisements again."

Jay didn't say anything for a long moment.

"Do you want to go with them?" Luci asked.

"I don't know. Don't you?"

"Yes. And that's what makes it so difficult."

"If either of us decides to go and the other one doesn't, the one who stays behind should feel no pressure to cover."

"That's a good deal."

"And there will be no hard feelings either way."

"Yeah."

Luci wondered if that would be as easy to do as it was to say. She felt that if she didn't go, the others would see her as a wuss.

But, on the other hand, what was so terrible about having them think this? She'd probably never see them again—except for Jay. But what if Jay thought she lacked a sense of adventure? That could ruin their friendship. Maybe they could still see each other, but it would change everything, would be an obstacle to deeper friendship.

Luci didn't want to be put in this position, didn't want to be forced to make this choice.

"You don't have any reservations about going out into the wilds of France in the middle of the night no matter how bright the moonlight?" Luci asked.

"Of course I do. But that's part of the adventure."

Luci stood up. If they didn't hurry back, Fran would be looking for them. "A cave? Going into a cave in the dark?"

Wasn't that something like going on the subway at night? It's something you never, ever do.

Jay got on her bike. "Maybe they'll back out."

"Logan? He'll have it all planned out by the time he gets back to the hotel."

This was such a beautiful little town and Luci had been enjoying this trip so thoroughly up until this afternoon. Now she felt uncomfortable. No matter what decision she made, she would feel wrong.

Maybe Glin was right. You only live once. But Luci wanted to keep living. It could be very dangerous going into a cave at night.

Would she do it for a million dollars?

"Do you think there could be a million dollars in the cave?" Luci asked.

"Could be."

"Do you think there's anything in the cave?"

"Could be."

"Do you think there are bats in the cave?" Luci

continued. "Bats and spiders? Big spiders with hairy legs. I hate spiders."

"Spiders sleep at night."

"Are you making that up, or did you learn that at your fancy school in Montreal?"

Jay smiled.

"You're saying that because you know there are really ugly spiders in that cave and they sleep all day."

Jay smiled.

"I bet spiders are really active at night," Luci grimaced and turned her bike into the hotel driveway.

She felt like writing a letter to her parents. Sort of a last will and testament.

Dear Mom and Dad—

By the time you read this, Getaway Tours will have notified you that my body has not yet been recovered but they are hoping to find it eventually. A detailed map has been made. . . .

Luci went to her luggage and got out a sheet of notepaper. She wouldn't say it so bluntly. After all, if she was lost in the foothills of the Pyrenees, they'd be upset.

They would also be arguing between themselves.

"I told you she was too young to go."

"I thought we had raised her to be more responsible! You can't blame me for her lack of judgment."

"I'm blaming you for your lack of judgment."

"You could have said no!"

"So could you!"

They'd be arguing about this trip forever.

Okay. Say it more tactfully.

Dear Mom and Dad—

You've been great parents and you shouldn't blame yourselves for this accident. It was . . .

Luci brightened. Temporary insanity! *Yes!* That was the one defense that always got everyone off the hook. She certainly couldn't claim it was a dysfunctional childhood.

Jay entered the room. "What are you smiling about?"

"Temporary insanity." Luci was nearly laughing.

"I didn't realize that was a laughing matter."

"It's not, of course. But if I go tonight, I can claim I lost my mind this afternoon. How else can I explain a decision like this?"

Jay sat on her bed. "You shouldn't stew about this. You're wasting a lot of energy. Either you want to go or you don't. It's not a big deal either way."

"Can you make up your mind that easily?"

"Yes."

Luci believed her. "Have you made it up yet?"

Jay shook her head.

"What would your mother say?"

"She wouldn't want me to put myself in any danger, but she's never been one to play it safe either."

"Marrying your father?" Luci asked.

"Not even that. Think about the chance she took moving to America. That meant leaving her family and friends to start a life in another country. That was a big gamble. We're still not sure it was the right thing."

"I guess going into a cave is small potatoes."

"When she was not much older than me, she was a singer."

"No! Was she famous?"

"Hardly. She sang backup for this sort of lounge singer who did Elvis songs."

"Not an Elvis impersonator."

"No. He did Engelbert Humperdinck and Tom Jones. Paul Anka, I guess. The three girls all wore the same wigs and the same little dresses. I saw pictures of her. It was a hoot."

"Did they ever play in America?"

"That would have been the big time. They played in all the nothing towns out in western Canada. Manitoba. Alberta. Saskatchewan. Doing a little routine behind the singer." Jay waved her arms, pointed, flounced.

"You've got it down perfectly."

"Sure. You should have seen me when I was five. I could have been on *Star Search*. Ugh."

Luci lay back on the bed. "I thought I was just going to be a sappy little American tourist dragging around France, looking at the sights, getting sore feet, and eating too much. This is so much more complicated."

There was a knock on the door. Jay stood and crossed to it. She opened it to Logan.

"Meet us on the terrace. I have the plan worked out." Logan walked down the hallway.

"A plan already," Luci moaned.

Glin and Logan were waiting on the terrace when Luci and Jay arrived.

"I have twenty minutes before the hardware store closes. I'm going to get everything we need to do this. We're going to need a long rope and a couple of flashlights. We'll need an ax or a hammer and a small shovel. Don't forget, we have to carry these things on our backs or tie them to the bikes."

Forget? Who but Logan would have thought of it?

"How deep is this cave?" Jay asked.

"I don't know," Logan said.

"Is the rope to tie to the outside so we can find our way back out again?"

"I don't think that's necessary," Logan replied.

"It sounds like a good idea to me," Luci said.

"I have a very good sense of direction," Logan assured them.

"Maybe you'll get disoriented," Luci countered.

"No, Luci. He's been flying his whole life. He always knows where he is."

"Does that apply to the ground as well as the air?" Jay asked.

"What if there are multiple tunnels? What if we go left and then right and then left. Who's going to remember all this? Why can't we leave a trail of cookie crumbs like Hansel and Gretel?"

"Popcorn."

Logan regarded them patiently. "We don't have popcorn."

"What about a long string? Get a ball of twine at the hardware store." Luci said.

"We'll tie ourselves together so we don't lose any of the company. I'll be the point man."

This was starting to sound like a military maneuver.

"What's a point man?" Jay asked.

"That's the most dangerous position. To take the lead is to put yourself at the greatest risk," Glin explained.

Luci stood up. "This doesn't sound good to me."

"What doesn't?" Stacey asked.

They all turned to see Stacey standing at the doorway in a fluffy white terry-cloth robe.

No one knew what to say. How much had Stacey heard?

"Bouillabaisse. Fish stew. It's very popular on the coast. It originated in Marseilles."

"It didn't sound like you were talking about food, Luci." Stacey had a suspicious look in her eyes.

"What did it sound like we were talking about?" Glin asked.

Stacey paused. "The way you ask makes it seem like you're covering something up. I wonder what that could be?"

"Nothing," Jay said.

"The way you four huddle together all the time puts a lie to that answer."

"What then?" Logan asked evenly.

Luci watched him. There wasn't a hint on his face that he was covering up anything.

"I'll have to think about it. I'm sure all the pieces are here, they just have to be put together in the right order. See you at dinner." Stacey went back into the hotel.

The group let out a collective sigh of relief.

"Do you think she can figure it out?" Luci asked.

"Count on it," Jay said.

Luci changed into better clothes for dinner. She had learned that the French were far more formal than Americans. People were supposed to dress for dinner, not just be clean and neat. It was good Luci had brought along a couple of outfits that had interchangeable pieces. Although she wasn't anywhere near as fancy as Stacey, she didn't feel out of place.

Jay sat in the overstuffed armchair and read until the last minute.

"Tell me about Sam," Luci said.

"You know everything you want to know about his family."

"What about him? What does he look like?"

"I can describe him in two words," Jay smiled. "Scrump tious."

Luci laughed.

"He's tall, has blue eyes, reddish-brown hair. It's very thick and a little wavy. He's athletic. They have a sailboat, so he's like a fish. He's on the swim team at school. He's very competitive. They send the team all over Canada for meets. Of course he plays tennis. It's something people of that caliber do."

Luci thought for a moment. "Is he like his parents at all? Isn't the expression 'the apple doesn't fall far from the tree'? How can you be raised in a family and not be like them at all?"

"I don't know. Sam is like his parents. He has social graces. That's something most people don't talk about anymore, but when you see it, you know it. His parents must be kind because he is."

"Do you miss him?" Luci asked.

Jay didn't answer.

"Does it bother you to talk about him?"

"I miss him, but I'm not sick at heart."

"He must care about you if he called your mother to ask about you."

"I'm sure he does."

There was a tap at the door. "It's me. Fran."

Luci went to open the door.

"We're gathering in the library for some noshes before dinner."

"Okay," Luci replied.

"Have you seen Logan?" Fran asked.

"Logan," Luci repeated. "Jay, have you seen Logan?"

"Uh. Not recently."

"I'm sure he's around someplace. Tim wanted to talk to him. See you downstairs in ten minutes."

Luci nodded as she closed the door.

"Have you made up your mind yet?"

Jay shook her head.

"Would you think I was a coward if I didn't go?"

"No."

"Maybe it's better if one of us doesn't go. If Logan has some kind of time frame for this escapade and he doesn't return, someone should know where he's gone."

Jay thought about that for a moment. "That sounds good, but won't that person who stays behind take an awful lot of heat should anything go wrong? That person would be blamed for not having come forward earlier."

Luci grabbed her purse. "I hate this." She opened the door and stepped into the hallway. "I hate this. I hate this."

Jay closed the door behind them.

Chapter Twelve

Luci walked into the library. Everyone was there but Logan. Best not to mention that.

"Where's Logan?" Stacey asked.

Fran glanced around the room. "I haven't seen him for several hours." She looked pointedly at Luci and Jay. "Someone must know where he is."

Logan? Logan who?

No one said anything.

"Glin?"

"He said something about checking out the hot springs. One of the maintenance men promised to show him the waters' source."

Tim took a slice of cheese. "Sounds like Logan."

"I don't care where the water comes from. It's fantastic. My skin is so soft since I've had the treatments, I wish I could take it home with me," Stacey commented.

Luci imagined Stacey's skin being so soft that it fell off her.

"So you've enjoyed your stay here?" Fran asked.

"Yes," Stacey admitted hesitantly.

"Well, the good times are far from over," Fran said. "The local theater company is staging a play tonight and we're all going. It's part of the celebration called *Les Médiévales*."

Luci forced a smile to her face.

"What are we seeing?" Jay asked.

"It's a retelling of the Parsifal legend," Fran replied. "It originated in this region and the people hold it very dear."

"I've never heard of it," Daria said.

Fran smiled. "Glin, would you like to illuminate us?"

"It's the story of the Holy Grail," Glin replied.

Jay inched closer to Luci. "We'll never get away tonight if we're going to be out late at the theater."

"Maybe that's for the best. Right?"

"What's a Grail? Is it a bird?"

"No, Daria. You're thinking of quail," Tim said.

"Oh yeah. Quail. We have those in California."

At that moment Logan rushed into the library carrying a large bottle. "Water!" he announced. "Sorry I'm late, but we had to trek up the mountain and it took longer than I thought it would. Did I miss anything?"

"No," Fran replied.

Luci wondered if Fran suspected anything. Some people might not have given it a second thought, but Fran was too smart and too young not to see the holes in Logan's story. Then again, he did have a bottle of water.

Which he could have gotten straight from the tap.

Maybe going to a play would be the perfect solution. There wouldn't be enough time to get into trouble.

"The Grail was the cup Jesus drank from at the Last Supper," Tim continued.

"So some people say. It could have been anything. The notion of a vessel possessing magical powers comes from the earliest written histories," Glin replied. "There are several references to magical caldrons in Celtic mythology."

Magic caldrons. Holy Grails. Terrific. All of this would just keep Logan fixated on going after the treasure.

Luci glanced at her watch hopefully. "Isn't it time for dinner?"

Fran stood. "So it is."

"You'd better tell us more about the Parsifal legend before we go to the theater," Fran said. "It won't be in English and I'm afraid most of us will be lost."

The *serveur* brought dessert to the table. Luci had ordered cherry *clafouti*, a light, custardy dessert containing fresh cherries. Jay had decided on a *tarte Tatin,* a pastry much like apple pie except there was only one crust. Fran had ordered the *crêpes suzettes,* a very thin pancake with an orange sauce. Daria had opted for *glace au chocolat,* chocolate ice cream, and the rest had chosen an almond *tarte*.

"Glin, before you start talking about the story, how

do you know so much about it?" Jay asked as she dug into the *tarte*.

"It's one of the courses my mother teaches at school. The Grail legend is a lifelong study because there are so many facets to it."

Luci tried to picture Mrs. Woods. Maybe she used her own name. She must be tall and attractive, since Glin was.

That was as far as Luci had been able to go. Did they live on a farm or in a log cabin or maybe some kind of ski chalet? It was Vermont, after all. Did they have all the modern conveniences or were they more ecologically minded and shunned things like electricity and running water? Maybe they lived in a burm house, partially underground, and they used solar panels for power. Maybe they lived in a gypsy caravan with colorfully painted walls.

Luci wanted to ask Glin all these things and more. But she never found the time or the way. In another few days the tour would be over and her chance to find out how Glin lived would be gone forever.

Tim held out a forkful of almond *tarte* for Fran. She held out a bite of *crêpes* for him.

Stacey sipped her water.

"The hero of the story is named Perceval. In German it's Parzival. Sometimes he's called the son of the widow lady. He leaves home to become a knight. During his travels, he meets Anfortas, the Fisher King, and is invited to stay the night in the castle. Perceval is supposed to ask a question, but he doesn't know what to ask. And because he doesn't ask whom one serves with the Grail, the whole country is plunged into a blight, a winter of their collective souls."

"If you serve with the Grail, is it a dish or a bowl?" Tim asked.

Glin smiled. "Or does it mean to serve as a knight would serve a king? Anyway, the castle disappears and Perceval goes out into the world. He fights many knights and does many heroic deeds, but forgets the Grail castle. One day, many years later, he remembers what he has forgotten." Glin stopped.

"Don't leave us hanging," Stacey said.

"That's where the original legend ended," Glin explained.

"Then what's the Grail?" Daria asked.

"Maybe the Grail is in us," Glin said. "We serve others with the gift of our self."

"So then all the quests searching for the magical Grail cup is a waste of time," Luci said.

"Only if you expect a real cup at the end of your journey," Glin told her.

Right then, Luci knew she had to go with them to the cave.

The play was fascinating. The costumes were marvelous, suggesting the craftsmanship once lavished on clothing. When Luci couldn't follow the action, Jay would softly translate for her. Although the scenery was sparse, Luci's imagination filled in all the blanks. She could picture King Arthur's court, the castle, the pageantry, the banners, the tapestry, the horses.

She was lost in thought the entire way back to the hotel. Before, all of those legends had just been more history to learn. Now she wanted to get to a library and read everything she could find on King Arthur, and the Middle Ages.

Perceval was treated to a feast. What was he served? Did they eat the same foods? How were they prepared? What kind of clothes did they wear? Were the costumes accurate?

Glin would know.

Maybe Luci could ask. It wouldn't be small talk, and whatever he told her had to be interesting. Maybe there would be time on the drive to Saint-Tropez.

They entered the hotel and Luci glanced at the hall clock. Almost eleven-thirty. There was no question in her mind. The treasure hunt was canceled.

She began to walk up the stairs.

"I guess we're staying in tonight," Jay said softly.

"I guess. Too bad."

"Were you going?" Jay asked in surprise.

"Yeah. I couldn't miss a Grail quest."

"But would you miss a quail quest?" Jay laughed.

They went down the hallway toward their room.

"Not quail. It can be very tender," Luci replied.

Jay opened the door.

Logan was striding down the hall. "Midnight on the terrace," he said into Luci's ear without stopping.

By the time the words registered, Logan was in his room.

Luci closed the door behind them and sat on the chair.

"What did he say?" Jay asked as she pulled off her sweater.

"Midnight on the terrace."

"He's still planning on going?"

"Sounds like it. What do you think? I don't know how long it'll take to get there and get back. Then we have the time searching in the cave. That could take six hours."

Jay nodded. "It would be dawn. Fran would be sure to see we were gone."

"This is very tricky."

"Not to mention possibly dangerous."

"Let's decide now so we can either go to bed or get ready for the adventure of a lifetime."

"Aren't you cheery."

"I figure if we go, we'll remember this night forever."

"And if we get caught?"

"We'll remember that, too."

Jay pulled her boots out of her bag. "If we survive."

That was something Luci was trying to push to the back of her mind. "I don't want to sound like your mother, but we should visit the ladies' room before we leave."

"Good suggestion. You go first. I'd better tie back my hair. I wouldn't want to get tangled up in roots or something."

Luci left the room. What was the other something Jay didn't want twisted up in her hair?

As she went down the hall, Luci heard a noise. She stopped. It was coming from the bathroom. She listened at the door.

Someone was crying.

Luci tapped on the door.

There was no answer, but the crying continued.

"Excuse me. Are you okay in there?"

"Who is it?"

"Luci."

There was no reply.

"Daria?" Luci asked.

"Yeah?" The voice was broken.

Luci tried the doorknob. It wasn't locked. "I'm coming in." Slowly she opened the door.

Daria was sitting on the floor surrounded by a mound of tissues.

Luci crouched beside her. "What's wrong?"

"I want to go home."

"The tour will be over in a couple days and then we'll all go home."

"No. I heard from my father. I'm not allowed to come home yet."

Luci sat on the floor beside her. "Why not?"

"I'm being punished."

"What did you do?"

Daria dissolved into tears again. Luci held out a wad of tissues for her.

There was a tap at the door. "Luci?"

"Jay, come on in."

Jay stepped inside. "You've been gone so long, I got worried. What's . . . going . . . on?" She looked at Daria sobbing. "What did Stacey do to you?"

"It's not Stacey." Daria gulped.

"She wants to go home," Luci explained. "And her father won't let her."

"What's he going to do, make you stay here by the side of the road?" Jay asked.

"No. I have to stay with my aunt in New York until

the next tour leaves. It's . . . it's . . . Indonesia!" Daria wailed.

"If you want to go home, go home. Show up on the doorstep. What's he going to do, lock you out?" Jay asked reasonably.

"He might."

Daria blew her nose into a tissue and dabbed at her eyes.

Luci handed her more tissues. "What did you do?"

"Yeah, can you apologize or anything?"

"That doesn't do any good. He's making a point," Daria explained.

"Can you promise you won't do it again?" Luci suggested. "Swear on your life? Cross your heart and hope to die or something?"

"You don't understand. With him, you never know. We were going . . ." Daria gulped. "We were going to a horse show in Oregon. We had just gotten past San Francisco. I told my sister that this one judge seemed to like Thoroughbreds more than quarter horses, and my mother agreed. My father started screaming."

"Why?"

"Because she took my side!"

Luci and Jay exchanged a look.

"Then he said just for that my mother had to drive all the way to Oregon without stopping. She was sniffing smelling salts for fourteen hours to keep from running the car off the road! My horse was in the trailer and I was scared we were all going to be killed. The minute I got home, he packed my bags and sent me to New York."

Jay sighed.

Luci didn't know what to say.

Jay reached out and put her hand on Daria's shoulder. "No one can make this better for you, and I'm not saying it's going to be easy. But I can tell you what someone told me when I was going through a bad time."

"What's that?" Daria sniffed.

"What doesn't kill you makes you stronger."

"And you believe that?"

"I know it," Jay replied. "Count the days until you go off to college. Pick the most expensive one you can find. Get straight A's," Jay added.

Daria smiled slightly. "That's only two years away."

"You can make it."

Daria nodded. "Yeah." She dumped the tissues into the wastebasket. "Thanks." She left the bathroom.

"Will she make it?"

Jay nodded. "If he's that tough, there must be enough of him in Daria to help her survive."

Luci sighed. "I've never felt luckier."

Jay glanced at her watch. "Yikes! It's after midnight!" She flew through the door with Luci close behind.

Chapter Thirteen

Luci and Jay rushed into their room.

"What do you think we need?"

Jay kicked off her shoes. "Boots. A sweater. Do you have gloves?"

"No." Luci dragged a sweater on over her head as she tried to get out of her shoes at the same time.

"Me neither."

"Do you think they've left already?" Luci said still caught up in her sweater.

"Maybe."

There was a knock at the door.

"Logan?" Jay asked Luci in a whisper.

Luci managed to get her head through the opening. "Who's there?"

"Fran."

Luci's mouth opened in surprise. Jay motioned at her to take off the sweater; otherwise it would be suspicious. They were supposed to be undressing for bed, not putting on heavy clothes.

Jay kicked the shoes under the bed as Luci tried to straighten her shirt. Jay opened the door.

Fran smiled. "I'm sorry to stop by so late, but I figured you two weren't in bed yet."

"Oh no, we were just—"

"Talking," Jay finished.

"Right."

Fran sat on the chair. "It's always nice when a real friendship develops on one of the tours. Some friendships last only for a month. Some last while you're in school. Some will last when you have a specific job. But finding a friend for life is really a blessing. I think that's the kind of friendship you've found."

Luci tried to make herself relax as she sat on the edge of her bed. "I think so." She felt as though she were going to jump right out of her skin. This was torture.

"And I want to thank you for the way you've been treating Stacey. I know you didn't connect with her, but she has something to offer."

"Absolutely," Jay said.

"It's important to make the effort to get along. You don't have to be best friends, but as long as you try to see the good in everyone, you'll take with you an enriched experience."

Luci nodded. "I've learned a lot from Stacey."

Jay glanced at her, straight-faced. "Yeah. I know much more about fashion than I ever thought possible."

Fran stood. "I'm glad we were able to agree to the

side trip. Stacey did make a concession for the rest of us."

"She's been great."

"Maybe next time it'll be your turn."

"I hope there is a next time," Luci replied honestly. She would be glad to go anywhere Stacey wanted to if there was another trip in her future.

Fran paused at the doorway. "I'm sure you'll enjoy Saint-Tropez, too."

"It must be very beautiful."

Luci tried not to squirm. Why wasn't Fran leaving? Wasn't Tim going to wonder where she was?

"I guess I'll say good night and stop by the boys' room and thank them, too."

"Uh . . ." Luci began.

"I think they're already asleep," Jay said.

"Really?" Fran asked in surprise.

Luci began turning down her bed. "Logan said that trek up the mountain for the water really tired him out."

"Exhausted," Jay added.

Fran laughed. "Amazing. Logan doesn't have un-limited energy, after all. I'll see them tomorrow. Good night, girls."

Fran left the room and Luci flopped onto the bed. "I thought she'd never leave!"

"Did it sound like she suspects something?"

"Yes. And I think I'm a hundred percent paranoid right now. You could ask me if the room is bugged and there are hidden surveillance cameras and I'd say yes to that, too!"

"Ssshh," Jay said as she listened at the door for a

moment then slowly and carefully opened it. She poked her head out. "Come on."

Luci grabbed her sweater, stuck her feet into her boots, and rushed out of the room.

"What time is it?"

"Ten after."

"They must have left."

Jay hurried down the stairs soundlessly.

Halfway down, Luci hit a step that creaked loudly. She froze, expecting every door in the hotel to open.

"Vite! Vite!" Jay whispered, telling her to hurry.

Luci tiptoed down the rest of the stairs as lightly as possible. "I thought you swore off French."

"I'll use it if it's convenient!"

They rushed to the back door.

"What if it's locked?"

Jay reached for the knob.

"What if it's got an alarm?" Luci asked, grabbing Jay's hand. She could imagine that the moment the knob was twisted, loud sirens would begin shrieking and searchlights would flood the area. They would be pinned down by the concierge holding a broom.

"Yes or no?" Jay asked.

Luci dropped her hand. "Yes."

Jay twisted the knob. The door opened silently. They went through and closed it behind them.

"I didn't think you were coming," Logan said out of the darkness.

"I persuaded him to wait fifteen minutes," Glin said.

"First it was Daria," Jay explained.

"Then it was Fran. We talked her out of going to your room."

"When?"

Luci got on her bike. "Now."

"Thanks," Logan said.

"Do you have everything?"

"Yes. Don't turn on your lights until we're on the street." Logan pushed off and headed down the driveway.

Luci thought it was very considerate of the French to have bicycles set up with lights for riding at night. While the lights wouldn't be as bright as headlights on a car, they would help a bit.

She pedaled quickly to keep up with the rest of them. All she could do was hope that they wouldn't be going too far—or the others would have to bring her back on a stretcher.

"I have two flashlights. They only had one at the hardware store. I got the other from the maintenance man."

"What about the rope?" Luci asked as she switched on her headlight.

"I got the rope. Twenty-five feet."

"Did you get anything to mark a trail?" Jay asked.

"No, I didn't. I said we didn't need it."

"I don't agree."

"Too late now," Glin pointed out. "We'll stay together and we'll remember which way we came."

Luci didn't love the sound of that. She was notoriously bad at directions. All that turn-left, turn-right stuff got very confusing. Especially in the dark.

Luckily she was going to be tied to the rest of them. If Logan was going to lead, did that mean Glin would bring up the rear? Was she going to be tied to him?

Luci had to pick up her pace to keep up. Logan was far ahead of them. The night was quiet except for the sound of the bicycle tires on the road and the gears going around.

She would never have imagined herself riding around the French countryside in the middle of the night. She would never have thought she'd be going off in search of an ancient treasure. This was definitely one of the best moments of her life.

Of course, it would be best if her parents never found out. They'd have her head on a platter. And Luci knew exactly which one. The Villeroy and Boch bone-china serving platter, an apple in her mouth, surrounded by parsley and perhaps some roasted potatoes.

No. Her parents should never hear a word about this.

"Luci! Are you still there?" Jay called back to her.

They had pulled ahead of her again. Thinking and pedaling didn't seem to mix.

"Still here."

"Well, don't get lost."

"Right," Luci replied as she picked up her pace to catch up with them.

Logan stopped his bike and shone the light on Georges's map. There was a road turning off to the right.

"Don't you know which way to go?" Jay asked.

"Yes."

"Then why have we stopped?" Jay asked as she

drew her bike closer so she'd be able to look over Logan's shoulder.

"Things look different on a map than they do in real life. Do you want to take the road to Lavaldieu instead?"

"No," Luci replied.

Logan pointed at the map so Jay could see where they were. "It's better to take the time to double-check than to go wrong."

"Time?" Glin asked.

"Twelve forty-five," Logan replied. "We should be close now." He replaced the map carefully and switched off the light. "I think it should be up the next hill."

They began pedaling again.

Luci hoped the cave would be right off the road, rather like a Popsicle stand. But she suspected they'd be trekking up the side of a mountain. Maybe she could just pull to the side and sit down until the rest of them had the adventure and came back.

No. She'd never forgive herself. Luci kept pedaling.

"I think this is it," Logan said as he got off his bike. "On the map it's called Point Bézu. The cave should be about fifteen minutes to the east."

Luci groaned inwardly. Fifteen minutes of hiking uphill?

Jay stepped closer to her. "It'll be downhill all the way back."

They began walking up the mountain. Logan carried one flashlight and gave Luci the other. Glin wore the backpack that contained the rope and the ax.

Luci pictured them as the seven dwarfs minus three.

Happy little miners going to work in their cave. She hummed their tune for a moment until she got too out of breath to continue.

"I figure we have three hours to search," Logan said. "It's taking us an hour to get there and an hour to get back."

"That's cutting it too close," Jay replied. "If everything goes perfectly, we'd get back at five. It'll be almost light by then. Someone will see us."

"Two hours isn't long enough," Logan countered.

"You don't know that," Glin replied.

They reached a small plateau. Logan looked skyward.

"What are you doing?"

"I'm looking for Polaris. The North Star."

Logan began pacing out steps to the north. The rest of the group followed him north and then east.

The moonlight was bright enough to make it possible to see each other as they picked their way over the rough terrain. There was no path to follow. It was very rocky, with squat bushes and grass the only vegetation.

"Time out," Luci said. "I need to sit down for a minute."

"I'm going on ahead, then," Logan replied.

Luci sat on a rock as Glin walked on also and Jay waited with her.

"Do you think there are any wild animals around?" Luci asked.

"Only Logan."

Luci retied one of her boots. "He's turning out to be better than I expected."

Jay sat nearby. "If you like going on commando missions."

"It *is* different."

"You don't think there's anything weird going on in the middle of the night that we didn't know about, do you?"

"Like what?"

"Bed checks?"

"I never thought of that. Fran would have to come into the room to check. I never heard a door open."

"Me neither."

"Don't you think that if there was ever a treasure, Saunière found it? That he spent it all?"

Jay thought about it for a moment. "It makes as much sense as anything else."

"Hey, ladies! Up here!" Logan called.

"We found it!" Glin shouted.

Luci and Jay raced up the mountain. Behind a large rock outcropping they saw the opening to a cave.

"Where's Logan?" Jay asked.

"He went in already."

"I thought we were in this together," Jay commented.

Logan stepped out of the cave. "We are. I just wanted to see if it was simply a crack in the rocks or something to walk in."

"Well?" Luci asked.

"Get the rope. We're heading in."

Glin removed the rope from his pack and unwound it.

Logan tied the rope around his waist. "Me. Jay. Luci. Glin. Okay?"

As the rope was being tied around her waist, Luci felt as if it was being tied around her neck. They were going into a very dark cave. A small dark cave.

Jay patted Luci's shoulder. "It'll be okay."

Luci took a deep breath.

Logan switched on the larger of the two flashlights. "Follow close behind." He handed Jay the other flashlight. "Hold it above my shoulder, pointed in the direction we're going. My light should cover the ground in front of us, yours will help with the distance."

"If there are any problems, stop and say something. Don't wait," Glin added.

Problems? What kind of problems? Was there an abyss inside? Was this like a Jules Verne story where they were going to fall to the center of the earth?

Or run into big hairy spiders who mutated from eating too much cheese rind.

Logan raised his hand and brought it forward. "Onward." He began walking and Jay followed. Luci felt a slight tug on her rope.

She didn't want to do this anymore.

"Come on, Luci," Jay said.

Luci stepped into the blackest black she had ever seen.

Chapter Fourteen

The thin beams from the flashlights barely penetrated the dark. Luci took each step hesitantly not being able to see where she was walking. She put her right hand out to feel for the wall, which was cool and damp. The ceiling was inches over their heads. The cave smelled of dry dirt, almost musty.

Luci began to feel claustrophobic. It was too dark, too close. She wanted to stop. She wanted some fresh air.

This wasn't like being in the fun house at an amusement park. There could be real danger here, not just a mechanical floor that vibrated at the flip of a switch. They weren't going to turn a corner and find themselves reflected in wavy mirrors. A plastic skeleton wasn't going to drop from the ceiling and say, "*Boo!*" Any skeletons they'd see were going to be real ones.

The rope tugged at her and she put one foot in front

of the other. If she bolted for the opening now, she'd be dragging Jay and Glin with her. Jay would understand. Glin might. Logan? No. Panic and fear would not go over well.

She tried to think of something else besides this tiny cave. Maybe it was a lot bigger than she imagined. It could go on for a hundred feet to her left and she'd never know.

She pictured bats hanging upside down and brushing her head with every step, their little bat wings all folded up tight.

No, Luci told herself. If it was night, bats would be outside flying around catching cows or goats. Wouldn't they?

One of the lights flickered.

"Hold it steady, Jay," Logan said.

Luci heard Jay rattle the flashlight.

"I was. It's doing it by itself."

This cave was altogether too silent. Luci could hear the dirt under their feet. She could hear the creak of their shoes and the swish of their clothing.

"Jay," Luci said.

"Uh-huh?"

"What's your favorite ice cream?"

"Umm. Peach." Jay sounded as if she were concentrating hard on walking forward.

"Glin?"

"Ginger."

"Interesting."

"Logan?"

"What?"

"What's your favorite flavor ice cream?"

"Geez, Louise. Chocolate. Glin, sing something before I'm asked what my favorite color is and what my dog's name is."

"Good idea," Jay agreed.

"Okay," Glin said, and paused, then he began singing.

"I was born and raised in East Virginia,
North Carolina I did go.
And 'twas there I spied a fair young maiden,
And her age I did not know.

"Oh, her hair was dark in color,
And her cheeks were rosy red,
And on her breast she wore a white lily,
Where I longed to lay my head.

"I would rather live in some dark hollow,
Where the sun refused to shine,
Than for you to be another man's darling
And to know you'll never be mine."

His voice echoed slightly in the cave, a haunting sound. "That's so pretty," Luci complimented, and instantly felt lame for saying something so lackluster.

"Does she die?" Jay asked.

"Jay!" Luci exclaimed.

"It sounds sad. Somebody has to die."

"No one dies," Glin said.

"Good choice," Logan commented. "I thought I could depend upon you to lighten things up a little."

"I'll know for next time."

Luci wanted this to be her first and only time in a cave.

The light ahead stopped, but Luci didn't and she bumped into Jay.

"Sorry."

"What's up?" Glin asked.

"There's a branch off to the right."

"I think we should always go straight ahead; that way we won't get confused."

"I don't think there's much danger of that."

"I do," Jay insisted.

"I vote for keeping it simple and uncomplicated," Glin said. "We can go straight in and then decide if we want to take any side trips on the way out."

Luci was impressed. He was much more diplomatic than she'd ever manage to be. "I agree."

"Okay," Logan said, disappointment showing. "Maybe."

They began to walk onward.

Luci wondered what time it was. She wondered how far they had gone already. She wondered how much farther they would go.

With her kind of luck, they'd come upon a bottomless pit, and as she looked over the edge the ground would crumble under her feet. Down she'd go like Alice in Wonderland. Falling forever with no Mad Hatter to keep her company.

"What if there's a chasm—" Luci started.

"Don't talk yourself into a tizzy," Jay said.

"Giant cracks in the earth appear only in cheap movies," Glin said.

"Think of this as a subway without a train," Jay said.

"Or muggers," Glin added.

"I don't want us to fall into a bottomless pit."

"That's not going to happen!" Logan said.

"That's right," Glin replied.

They stopped again as Logan checked the tunnel to the left. Luci felt something brush her face and gasped. "It's a bat!"

"No. It's me," Glin said. "I wanted to see the turnoff."

Logan shone the light down the tunnel. "I think we should go this way."

"Why?" Jay asked.

"Because we'll have more clearance. The ceiling's higher. This tunnel is narrowing too much."

"Then let's turn," Luci interjected.

"The deal was that we were going in straight," Jay said.

"What if we can't go much farther this way?" Glin asked.

"Then we turn around," Jay replied.

Luci imagined them getting stuck in the cave, unable to go ahead and unable to go back. "Let's turn."

"That's two votes for turning," Logan said. "Who'll cast the deciding vote?"

There was silence.

"Do you really think we won't remember when we turned left?" Logan asked.

"Yes," Jay replied.

"Then leave something here," Logan suggested.

"I told you to bring popcorn," Jay said.

Glin reached into his pocket and removed a coin, which he flipped onto the ground. "There's our marker."

"Satisfied?" Logan asked.

Jay shrugged. "Barely."

They began walking again, turning left down the more promising tunnel.

Luci wondered about the last time anyone had been in this cave. Had the Cathars run through this tunnel, fearing they were being followed by soldiers? Had the German miners been the last to have plumbed these depths? Was this a cave Georges had explored?

"Are there any footprints in the dirt?" Luci wondered out loud.

Jay swung her flashlight to the ground. "Not that I can see."

"Maybe no one's ever been in here," Luci said.

"Georges has been all over this terrain. I think he's been in every cave," Logan replied. "Why don't you try a little positive thinking?"

Luci thought for a moment. "Like affirmations? I saw someone on television talking about that. You repeat a statement over and over until it comes true. I will win the lottery. I will win the lottery."

"Yeah, something like that," Logan replied.

Suddenly Logan's light took a wild dip. "Ooff!"

"What?"

They all froze in place.

"I tripped over something."

Logan cast his light to the ground. It was a small log. "Does that answer everyone's concerns that no one has ever been in here before?"

"It didn't get here by itself," Glin admitted.

"At least we know someone has been here," Logan said.

"What if they're still here? French desperadoes hiding from Interpol."

"Luci, positive thinking," Jay said.

"If someone was in here now, there'd be footprints, right?" Logan pointed out.

Luci nodded. She was almost getting used to this. Being in so much dark was disorienting. There were no points of reference except for the beams of light. It seemed like a dream.

"Hold on!" Logan shouted.

Luci stopped abruptly.

"This looks like a chamber," Logan said as he played the light around the walls of the cavern.

Jay shone her light up and down. "It's a room."

Logan began untying the rope from his waist. "This is it! This must be Georges's cave!"

Luci glanced around the room. It was about twenty feet long by about twelve feet across. There was enough space to contain a lot of gold. Unfortunately, the room was empty. There wasn't a chair or a stick of wood or a treasure chest.

Logan began to shine the light along the wall, searching.

"What are you looking for?"

"Some kind of marking, or evidence that someone has been nearby."

"If they hid a treasure here, would they have painted an arrow on the wall pointing to it?"

"No. I don't expect that." Logan's nose was almost on the wall as he moved inch by inch.

"What's that?" Jay asked as she went to the wall and pointed. "This. It's a line. Here's another."

Logan shone the other light on the spot.

"It looks like a discoloration of the rocks," Glin said.

"It looks like a triangle," Luci said.

"No . . ."

"What did Georges say? The Cathars used a pentagram, right?" Glin said.

Luci traced the five lines on the wall. "That's what this is!"

"Pass the shovel over," Logan called out to Glin.

Glin opened his pack and took out a small shovel and an ax. Logan grabbed the shovel, dropped to his knees, and instantly began digging in the dirt.

"Wait a minute!" Jay said.

"Why?"

"Because you may be covering up a clue by throwing all that dirt around."

Jay shimmied out of the rope and dropped on her knees beside him. She began sifting through the dirt.

Glin untied himself and went to dig with them.

Luci stood there in the semidark, rope still around her waist, feeling useless. She didn't have a flashlight and she didn't have a tool for digging.

She sat down on the ground and her hand dropped to the dirt. Luci felt something smooth under her finger, but couldn't see anything in the dim light. Her fingers probed the soft earth for the object until it was loose. She picked it up and held it close to her face.

Even in the dim light, she could see that it was gold.

"Guys . . ." Luci started.

"What?" Logan asked without looking at her.

Luci held the object out between her thumb and forefinger. It couldn't have been more than an inch long, but its design was obvious. It was a bee.

"Is this what you're looking for?"

Instantly Jay grabbed her flashlight and shone it at Luci.

The gold bee glinted in the light.

There was a mad scrambling as they all tried to get to Luci. The shovel and ax were dropped. In the tight space, Glin bumped into Jay, who in turn bumped into Logan. His flashlight was thrown from his hand. When it hit the ground, it went out.

Logan picked up the flashlight and shook it. Nothing.

He began to unscrew the top.

"What are you doing?" Jay asked.

"Fixing it."

"Don't take it apart," Jay told him.

"We need it. Hold your light over here."

"Yessir. Right away, sir. Anything you say, *sir*."

"I didn't mean it like that. It wasn't an order."

"It sounded like one."

"I apologize up the Alps and down the Pyrenees. I would have said it the same way to Glin."

Jay wasn't convinced.

"Seriously, Jay," Glin assured her. "That's Logan's normal tone of voice in an emergency."

"Hmmm. Okay. Don't let it happen again."

"I promise. Just please shine the light on my flashlight."

Jay brought the beam around to Logan's hands.

Logan removed the bulb.

Jay's flashlight grew dimmer and dimmer. "I'm not doing that."

"Shake it or something."

Jay shook the flashlight. The light flickered.

"Logan . . ." Luci began.

Logan reached for the working flashlight, but Jay pulled it away from him.

"You've already wrecked one!" Jay exclaimed.

"I'm fixing it!"

"That's what guys always say when the thing is in a million pieces! Then it never works again."

"You fix it, then," Logan told her, sitting back.

"Jay . . ." Luci began.

"Yes, Luci?"

"Maybe it just needs to be tightened a little," Luci suggested cautiously.

"Just don't waste a lot of time thinking about it," Glin said.

Jay tightened the two pieces of the flashlight more firmly together. The light turned more yellow, more faint.

"That's a dead one," Logan commented.

The light went out.

They were in total darkness.

Chapter Fifteen

"**N**ow what do we do?" Luci asked, trying to remain calm.

There was no reply.

"You guys are still here, aren't you?"

"Sorry, Luci," Glin replied. "I was just thinking."

"Can we just walk out of here?"

"How?" Jay asked.

"Just feel along the wall and walk real fast."

"We made those turns. I don't think we should walk around in the dark," Jay said. "We could get lost."

"I can fix the flashlight," Logan assured them.

There was silence.

"I can," Logan repeated.

"I think I'm walking out of here." Luci stood. "I'll meet you all on the outside."

"Don't go," Jay said. "We'll get the flashlight to work. Somehow."

"No, no. I think I'll just take a little walk."

The more they talked about it, Luci thought, the smaller the room seemed to become. In a minute it would be no bigger than a dollhouse.

"I have a lighter," Logan said as he tried to get it out of his pocket.

"What else do you have?" Jay asked.

"A Swiss army knife. We can fix anything."

"What are we going to do for light so we can see to fix all these things?" Jay asked.

"We'll take off the clothes we don't need and burn them," Logan decided.

"I don't think so," Jay replied.

Luci slipped the bee into her pocket then put her hand against the wall. "How many turns did we make?"

"You can't make it alone," Jay told her.

"Here's the lighter." There was a snap and a small flame sprang to life.

"Stick around," Glin said.

Luci shook her head. It was too late. Even the small flame didn't reassure her enough to make it possible to stay in the chamber a moment longer.

Glin stood. "I'll go out with you."

Logan looked up from the flashlight pieces. "What about the digging?"

"I'll dig," Jay said.

"Okay. It's a right turn two passageways down."

"I thought it was one."

"It's two."

"Look for the coin in the dirt."

Luci began walking. One turn. Two turns. What about that tunnel on the right—or was it the left?

Within a half-dozen steps, it was so dark Luci couldn't have seen an elephant in front of her face.

There was a touch on her arm, then Glin took her hand. "We'll go out together."

His hand was strong and warm. Luci felt safer immediately.

Glin paused. "Ten minutes."

"Be serious," Logan replied.

"That is serious. You don't need any more time than that."

Logan wanted to negotiate. "Times three."

"Not thirty minutes, Logan. Ten." Glin began walking and Luci followed him.

The return trip turned out to be more difficult than Luci had imagined. Not being able to see anything made her disoriented. She felt at times that the ground was rising beneath her feet. At other times she felt dizzy, that she was tilted or walking on the side of a hill.

"How are you doing?" Glin asked.

"Better with every step."

"This treasure hunt probably wasn't the best idea."

"No, it was a good idea if we could have been outfitted a bit better." Luci pictured an African safari with four-wheel-drive Land Rovers, water tanks, huge tents, a portable electric generator, and possibly a satellite dish. Clothes by Banana Republic. Stylish khaki, cool linens, hundred-percent cotton slouch socks, and hiking boots. A brown belt and a nice hat would complete the look.

She could almost hear the trumpet of the elephants

in the distance. "Bwana! Bwana!" someone would shout as they opened the flap to the tent.

What did *bwana* mean, anyway? That was never explained in those old Tarzan movies. But the English really knew how to travel. Not like the Americans, who were completely unprepared except for several rolls of good toilet paper.

Glin paused.

"What's wrong?"

Glin patted the wall. "There's another tunnel here."

"Is it the turn?"

"I don't think so."

Think? He didn't know?

What did Logan say? Pass the first two tunnels and take the third? How had he expected them to see the coin in the dirt? She couldn't even see Glin.

Glin began walking again.

"People do this for fun?"

Glin had her hand firmly in his. "So I've heard."

"Maybe I'm spoiled. I expect sidewalks and street signs. I guess I wouldn't have made much of a pioneer woman."

"I think you would have been fine."

"No. I read about those people on the Oregon Trail. They had to dig the wagons out of the rivers and gather weeds to eat. When they weren't cold and wet, they were roasting with the heat. Most of the time they had to walk. I can't imagine walking from Missouri to the Pacific Ocean."

"I think you could do anything you wanted to."

"What would make you think that?" Luci blurted out.

"You found the treasure."

"I sat on it!"

"You seem to have a fair degree of determination."

"Thank you, but I don't know if it's true."

"The more you test it, the more you'll see it." Glin paused again. "Another tunnel."

"This is the turn."

"Is it?"

"Yes." Luci surprised herself. Was she really so sure? "Let's look for the coin." She knelt down in the dirt and began patting the earth with her hands.

Glin knelt down beside her. "I don't think we can find it this way."

"I have good luck with this method."

He laughed. "Yeah, you do."

"This is something you probably don't know about me but my fanny has twenty-twenty vision."

Glin laughed.

Unable to see, she patted her hand over his. She moved her hand quickly. "Sorry."

"For what?"

Umm . . . For touching his hand unintentionally. And liking it. A lot.

Glin took her hand.

"What?"

"I'm not sorry."

She could feel him leaning over toward her. The spicy scent washed over her.

Was he going to kiss her?

Luci couldn't believe it.

She couldn't breathe.

His shoulder pushed into hers. Balance precarious, over she went.

"Luci?" Glin asked in surprise.

"The coin!" Luci felt under her hand for the round metal.

"You found it?"

Luci held it up, although she couldn't see it. "Got it!" It must have been a French franc because it didn't feel like an American quarter.

"Then we're going in the right direction."

He took a hold of her hand and helped her to her feet. "Let's book."

"You'll get no argument from me."

She quickly pushed the coin into her back pocket as she went with him. The coin would be a remembrance of this night, of this trip. Something of his that she could keep for herself.

The only person on the trip who had been taking photographs was Daria, and Luci and the rest had avoided having their pictures taken in any of the standard tourist poses.

Tim had taken a photo of the whole group standing on the ramparts at Carcassonne. Perhaps Luci could get a copy from him. Then she could frame it and put it on her nightstand with the coin right in front of it.

She felt it would be strange looking at Glin while she was in New York, imagining him in Vermont, separated not only by miles but by lifestyle.

They hurried down the tunnel so quickly that Luci's fingers were scraped by the rocks as she held her hand against the wall. She began to worry that she should have left the coin so Logan and Jay could have used it as a marker. But they would have the flashlights, and Logan was so sure of himself, he wouldn't be looking for a franc on the ground.

"I see light!"

"Are we at the end?"

"I think so."

Luci felt relief and joy at the same time. In a huge last stride she left the cave and found herself back on the mountainside. She took a deep breath of clean, fresh air.

"We did it!" Glin exclaimed raising his arms into the air triumphantly.

"Hallelujah, our butts are saved!" Luci shouted, and raised both her hands.

They slapped their hands together in a gleeful high five.

Slowly, Glin took her hands and drew her closer to him, until her body was next to his. He brought his arms around her, holding her tight.

She felt dizzier than when the floor of the cave seemed to be tilting and rolling under her feet.

She felt his breath on her neck. His hair soft against her cheek. His legs strong against hers.

"Luci," he whispered, pulling back slightly.

As she was about to say his name he pressed his lips against hers.

For an instant it was as though she had fallen through a tear in the fabric of time, tumbling into realm of soft, billowing sensation. Everything she felt was within her. The shell of her body had disappeared. There was no moon, no stars, no sky, no rocks, no ground beneath her feet. There was only the free fall into a new world.

It could have been five seconds. It could have been five centuries.

He raised her hand to his lips.

"Guys?"

Luci jumped, startled.

Glin didn't let go of her hand.

"No treasure," Logan reported as he dumped the shovel at the cave's entrance. "Not that I could find in ten minutes."

"We dug down deep," Jay added, coming out behind him.

"You would have thought it was one of those game shows where you can win a million bucks if you do some crazy stunt. Dirt was flying everywhere." Logan spit some dirt out of his mouth, then bent over and ran his fingers through his hair.

Jay tried to brush the dirt off her clothes. "I'm filthy, huh?"

"Not compared to a warthog," Luci confirmed.

"Well, with any luck, we'll get in without being noticed and you can take a shower before anyone wakes up. What time is it?"

Glin looked at his watch. "Two forty-five."

Logan took the ax from Jay and put it in the backpack. "Plenty of time. You've still got the treasure, Luci?"

Luci pulled her hand out of Glin's and patted her front pocket. "Right here."

"Okay. Then I guess we're ready to call this

played," Logan said as he started down the mountain-side.

"Did he ever get the flashlight working?" Luci asked Jay.

"Oh yeah. Right after you left. Then he fixed mine. Worked much better than it did before."

Luci and Jay followed Logan down the hill. "How deep did you go?"

"I'll bet we dug a hole three feet wide and two feet down."

"Nothing?" Glin asked.

"Nope," Jay replied.

"Doesn't really make any sense, does it?" Glin asked. "Luci finds something laying on top of the dirt."

"Maybe you should have dug there."

"We did. The chamber looks like the craters of the moon now. I have blisters on both hands."

"I should have stayed to help," Luci said.

"You didn't feel comfortable in there. Not that I can blame you. It was pretty creepy. Besides, there weren't enough tools for all of us."

Glin offered his hand to both of them as they came to a steep and rocky part of the path.

Logan was already at the bicycles, packing up. Glin made his way to the road.

"Did you look for the coin Glin left on the way in?" Luci asked.

"No. We didn't have time, why?"

"I took it with me."

"Why?"

Luci paused. "It was Glin's."

"So what was going on up there, *chère*?"

Luci shrugged.

"Does that mean you don't know?"

"No. It means I don't know how to put it into words."

"Oh."

"I don't want to make more of it than it was."

"What was it?"

"A kiss . . . between friends . . . who had just had a harrowing adventure."

"Uh-huh," Jay replied evenly as she followed the path to the road.

"Nothing more than that."

"Didn't say it was."

"These things shouldn't be overblown."

"I agree completely."

They reached their bicycles.

"We've got to hustle butt all the way back," Logan told them.

Jay nodded, too tired to make any comments.

They began pedaling down the hill.

Chapter Sixteen

After being in the dark of the cave, the moonlight seemed like high noon. Logan was far ahead of the others, disappearing around a curve in the road.

"What's with him?" Jay asked Glin.

"Very competitive," Glin replied.

"Bicycle racing?" Jay asked.

"No."

"You mean like Iron Man contests?" Luci asked, picturing Logan swimming a hundred miles through the ocean only to race up the beach and pedal a hundred more miles on a bicycle and then finish off by destroying an entire town with his bare hands. Godzilla had nothing on Logan.

"No. And don't give him any ideas."

"Does he ever relax?"

"Not often. Not in the way the rest of us mean relax.

Last summer we went sailing. We raced every time we went out. Of course we were with his father."

Luci's curiosity was getting the better of her. "What's his father like?"

"A bigger, older version of Logan."

"Have you been friends with Logan a long time?" Jay asked.

"About three years. We met on a river. He was white-water rafting with his father. I was there with my father."

"Rafting?"

"No. Protesting a decision to build a nuclear power plant on the river. There were lots of people camped out that weekend. It was sort of like Woodstock, but political. Everyone was there. The conservationists and the capitalists and the journalists. The Rainbow People were there."

"Who are they?" Jay asked.

"Hippies," Luci said.

"I guess you could say that," Glin admitted. "They look like hippies or Dead Heads."

"Followers of the Grateful Dead," Luci added.

Jay smiled. "I knew that."

"So anytime you draw a group like that, the media has to cover it. Sticking cameras in your face and asking dumb questions."

"Were you arrested?" Luci asked.

Glin paused. "Yeah. But everyone was."

"Logan, too?"

"It was . . . Logan got into this . . . discussion . . . with one of these Rainbow People who was not in a very good mood to begin with. Then there was some pushing. Which would have been fine except that *A Current Event* was there trying to get a story for their evening gossip show. They stuck their camera in Logan's face and he didn't like that. What with the name-calling and pushing and people falling in the river and in the mud, it's really hard to say who started it."

"Then the police came," Luci prodded.

"Once they dug themselves out of the mud and managed to get the tires back on the patrol car, they came right away."

"Is any of this true?" Jay asked.

"All of it," Glin replied. "You don't know what it's like in the Northeast Kingdom. It's a different world."

"What's Northeast Kingdom?"

"Is that a real place or is it in Dungeons & Dragons?"

Logan smiled. "Northeastern Vermont. We've very independent out there."

"Are you planning on seceding from the continental U.S.?" Luci asked.

"Not yet."

"So tell the story. What happened then?"

"After my mother finished bailing us out of jail—"

"She must have loved that, being a college professor and all," Jay remarked.

"That wasn't a problem where she teaches. It's a very progressive atmosphere. Students and faculty are encouraged to take action. You learn by doing."

Jay shook her head in amazement. "I want to check this place out."

"You should," Glin told her. "We got out of jail, wet

and muddy and cold. My mother brought us all home and put us in front of a huge fire."

"Burned you at the stake?" Luci teased.

"Gave us some soup and bread and dry clothes. We talked for a couple hours and adopted each other. The Carlisles have been part of our family ever since."

Luci felt a twinge of jealousy. Being a part of the Woods family sounded wonderful. It sounded so . . . picturesque to huddle around a huge fire, blankets draped around everyone's shoulders, telling stories, sharing food and life. That wasn't a scene likely to be played out anywhere in Manhattan.

"Logan's father will fly him up to Vermont when he has the chance and we get to visit. Sometimes I can get to wherever Logan is. Like last summer on the ocean."

"Did you ever get up to Montreal?"

"Oh sure. Montreal is really the largest city around. We go shopping there sometimes."

Luci couldn't imagine that. "You go to Canada to shop?"

"We're not driving to New York or Boston. Even Albany's farther."

"That's nothing, Luci. People in Montreal drive to Vermont to grocery-shop," Jay said.

"Why?"

"Remember what I said about butter being three dollars a pound? It's a dollar over the border. You save up, you get a friend with a big car, and off you go."

"You did that?"

"Sure. It was an all-day outing, but it's worth it if you want to save money."

"The farthest we go is over the river. There's a big outlet mall in New Jersey."

"Does your family have a car?" Jay asked.

"No. What would we need a car for?"

"Getting around."

"That's why mass transit was invented. If you want to go farther than greater metropolitan New York, you can take a bus or train. We've rented a car. My father and mother know how to drive."

"Do you?"

"No. But I'm sure I'll get my license someday. I don't really need it now, do I?"

"Have you ever driven?" Glin asked.

"No. I just turned sixteen anyway."

"Out in Vermont, kids drive when they're thirteen, fourteen."

"It's legal?"

"No," Glin admitted. "I'm not saying you have to drive on the highway. You just go out to learn, have some fun."

"Drive the tractor?" Luci asked.

"That, too."

"Do you have a tractor?"

"How else are we going to get the firewood out of the forest? We don't have a very large draft horse."

Luci tried to imagine Glin driving a tractor.

"And you chop wood?"

"Most people have a log splitter. Chopping wood is too much like work. There's an old saying. Wood heats you three times: when you cut down the tree, when you split the wood, and when you finally burn it in the fireplace."

Luci shook her head. He didn't seem like the woodsman type. "And what do you wear?"

"You mean like plaid flannel shirts and rubber boots?"

"Yes."

"That's what you wear to work outside in the winter. With flannel-lined jeans, of course."

"Serious?"

Jay bit her lip to keep from laughing. "You've been in the city too long, girlfriend."

"I thought it was just on TV. And Ralph Lauren advertisements. But who believes any of that stuff?"

"What did you think people wear to work outside?" Glin asked.

Luci was stumped. "I can't say I really thought about it." She knew from the very beginning that their worlds were too far apart. Did she seem hopelessly citified? Glin must think she was an idiot.

"No reason why you should have," Glin admitted.

They followed a curve in the road and Logan was waiting for them. Les Thermes was up ahead, a few dots of light on the dark hill.

"Let's get our story straight now in case anything happens."

Luci felt a catch in her throat. Getting caught seemed more real now than it had earlier. Of course Glin and Logan would be less concerned about getting stopped by Fran. They had been arrested and spent time in jail. Getaway Tours would hardly incarcerate their clients no matter what they did.

"Why don't we try telling the truth?" Jay suggested.

"Fine," Logan said. "Let's all tell the same truth."

"Are we going to leave something out?" Luci asked.

"Going into the cave is probably best left unsaid," Glin commented.

"Where have we been?" Jay asked. "If we have hours unaccounted for, someone may well suspect—"

"More intimate activities than spelunking. I don't want to get—"

"A reputation," Jay finished.

"Be serious," Logan said. "Who would think we'd be out here doing anything intimate?"

"Duh, Logan. Everyone," Luci replied in amazement.

"We deny it."

"What planet are you from? Kids who have been fooling around in the moonlight are expected to deny it!"

Luci could imagine Fran calling up her parents and reporting that Luci had spent the night with a guy. That would not go over well at all. Why hadn't she thought of that before?

Because she had been worried about falling into a crack in the earth.

Plunging to China would have been better than having to explain to her parents that yes, she had been with two very attractive young men alone, but nothing had happened.

Who would believe that? Not even Bozo the Clown.

Forget about being grounded for life. She'd be grounded for her next life, too.

"How would your mother feel about this, Jay?"

"I think she'd be very surprised."

Surprised is all?

"Glin? This would be okay with your parents?"

"My parents believe me. If I said nothing happened, they would accept it. I don't lie to them."

"Then what about leaving out the part about going in the cave?"

"I won't leave that part out when I tell them. I just don't know that we should volunteer that information to Fran and Tim."

Luci shook her head. "If we get caught, I think we should come clean. Tell the whole story. Throw ourselves on their mercy. We're stupid teenagers."

"Speak for yourself," Logan said.

"I'm not saying we are. I'm saying that that's how we will be seen and it can work in our favor. Bad judgment is expected of teenagers. They'll be mad, but we can apologize and all."

"I'm not into confessing," Logan stated firmly. "If they know something and have evidence, that's a different story. I'm not handing them the goods."

"This is turning into an ethical issue," Glin pointed out. "I don't think we need to go into our moral philosophies here. Let's just decide what we're going to say."

Logan was balancing on the bicycle. "*If* we get caught."

"Right. If."

"You two are dirty," Luci said. "We haven't been out for a bike ride in the moonlight."

"We hit some sand on the road and fell down. Simple," Logan replied.

"Fine," Luci said, and gave the bike a push. "You do

the talking, Logan. I'll stand there like a zombie. I'm too tired to argue about it anymore."

"Try a little positive thinking, Luci!" Logan called down the road.

The closer she got to town, the more nervous Luci became. Letting Logan do the talking was definitely a mistake. Then everyone would think she agreed with him. And she didn't.

If they were caught, she'd tell the truth, eventually.

On the other hand, what was so bad?

Going into a cave at night.

Leaving the hotel at night in a foreign country without adult supervision.

Being alone with two young men at night in a foreign country in a dark cave.

Any of those could be considered real breaches of good behavior.

They wouldn't cut the tour short, would they? The return tickets wouldn't be valid for an earlier date. Unless Getaway Tours could pull strings and have the booking changed.

Glin pedaled up beside her. "I don't think you should worry about this."

"Are you an old hand at these situations?"

"I've gotten into trouble before, if that's what you mean. Just think about it in terms of what you've gained. If you think going out tonight wasn't a life experience you'll remember and cherish for the rest of your life, then it won't be worth it. If you think this was important to you, it doesn't matter what else happens."

"Was this important to you?"

"I wouldn't have gone if it wasn't something I wanted to do. You don't regret what you've done as much as what you haven't done."

"I don't know that I believe that. I think there are plenty of things you can regret doing."

"This isn't one of them for me."

The hotel was just up ahead.

Luci wondered if she wasn't as adventurous as the rest of them.

She pedaled the bike up to the back of the hotel. Logan and Jay were waiting for them in the darkness. There were no lights on inside except for those left on at night.

"Okay?" Logan asked.

"I guess so."

He opened the door and they all walked in as carefully as possible. Logan paused in the corridor. There wasn't a sound in the hotel. Everyone was asleep.

They had done it. Gotten back without being detected.

Luci just wanted to crawl in bed and sleep for a couple hours. She was sure this would all seem quite different once the sun was up.

They tiptoed along the hall past the library.

"So you guys finally got back." Fran flipped on the light switch.

Tim was stretched out in a big wing chair.

"Get in here," Fran commanded, and they all went into the library. "I am so angry with you I can barely keep myself from bopping your heads together. Where were you?"

Logan pulled himself up. "We were—"

"You." Tim pointed at Logan. "Keep. Quiet."

Luci shrank inside. This could be worse than she imagined.

Fran pointed at Luci. "You tell me the story."

Logan opened his mouth to speak and Fran glared at him.

"Logan, I can't trust you. I thought you had more sense. But guess what? I was wrong. Start talking, Luci."

Luci shifted her weight from one foot to the other. Logan, Glin, and Jay were looking at her. "Okay. So we were at the market and I picked up some strawberries. I didn't know you weren't allowed to touch anything. The shopkeeper went ballistic and was yelling at me in French, but I couldn't understand a word of it."

Tim crossed his legs. "I hope this gets better, because it's real weak right now."

"This old guy came along and made it all right with the shopkeeper. Isn't that right, Jay?"

Jay nodded.

"We went out on the street and told him where we had been and all. He tells us to go to Rennes-le-Château and then come back to him."

"That's why we went there?" Fran asked.

"Yeah. So the next day we go to his cottage and he convinces us that he has this map to where the Cathar Treasure is."

"You guys aren't too gullible," Tim remarked. "When'd you fall off the turnip truck?"

"He gave us the map that Saunière had made."

Logan pulled the map out of his pocket and held it up as evidence.

Fran took the map and studied it.

At that moment Stacey and Aimee entered the room.

"I heard all this noise; what's going on?" Stacey asked. "You been taking a mud bath?" she asked Jay. "The point is to take your clothes off *before* you get in the mud."

"Thanks. I'll try to remember that," Jay replied.

Aimee smiled at everyone and sat on the arm of a chair, pulling her huge sweatshirt around her.

Fran held out the map. "This is in the mountains."

"Yeah. In the mountains. We went there on the bicycles."

"You know it's against the rules to leave the hotel at night?" Fran asked.

Luci paused for a long time. "Can I come back to that question? Logan planned it all out and got the equipment we'd need."

"Figures," Tim commented.

"I didn't really want to go into the cave—"

"You dodobrains went into a cave?" Stacey exclaimed.

"Stacey, that's enough," Fran said.

"Did you at least have flashlights?" Stacey asked.

"Logan got one from the hardware store and one from the maintenance man, but that one didn't work very well. It went out. After Logan tripped over the good one and it fell apart."

"What is this? The Marx Brothers Go Exploring?" Stacey asked.

"I guess they don't make flashlights in France the way they do in America. Although they're all probably made in Malaysia or someplace where people don't use flashlights."

"Luci . . ."

"So we're in the cave and I sat down. And I found this." Luci took the bee out of her pocket and held it out in the palm of her hand. "It looks like gold."

Fran stepped closer as the others gathered around Luci to view the object in the light.

"What is it?" Tim asked.

Aimee picked the bee up and turned it over. "The symbol of the Merovingian dynasty was a bee. When one of the tombs was opened, out fell all these gold bees. They say that for Napoléon's coronation cloak, over three hundred ancient bees were sewn onto the cloth. They've disappeared now. But this looks real similar."

Daria stood at the doorway. "Who are the Merovingians?"

Aimee handed the bee to Logan. "Merovingians preceded everyone in this region. What . . . about 500 A.D.?"

"About that," Glin replied.

"What did Saint Rémy say to Clovis when he was being baptized?

" 'Revere what thou has burned and burn what thou hast revered.' Something along those lines."

Luci looked at Glin in amazement. "How do you know that?"

"It's a very famous quote. Clovis was a major military leader of his era. He took over the Frankish kingdom when he was about sixteen and went on to conquer most of Northern Europe."

"He was the first of the Frankish pagans to be baptized into Roman Christianity," Aimee said, smiling. "It didn't really take, though. He remained loyal to the Cult of Arduina until he died. A goddess cult. My mother has a thing for goddess cults."

Logan turned the bee over in his hand. "So Saunière opened up the pillar and found . . . ?"

"Something left by the Cathars which pointed the priest in the right direction," Luci said.

Logan nodded. "With the information in hand, he searched the countryside until he found the Cathar Treasure."

"Right," Glin said. "And left part of the treasure there for his housekeeper's use."

"This new map was for her," Luci finished.

Daria sat next to Stacey. "I'm so confused."

"Who cares about all these dead people anyway?" Stacey interjected.

"Guys, guys. There's no treasure," Tim said.

"Explain this gold bee," Logan demanded.

"Probably a trick this old man is playing on you. He could well put this in the cave and wait for naive tourists to go off on a wild-goose chase. He's probably at home laughing his head off," Fran said.

Luci shook her head. "He can't walk from here to the corner. He's not going to go hiking up a rocky mountain just to play a joke on some tourists."

"It takes all kinds," Tim commented.

"As shown by your actions tonight," Fran said.

"So . . . what's the deal? Are we going to be beheaded at dawn?" Logan asked.

"I don't know. I'm glad you're all back safe and sound, but it was really dumb. I have to think about this. Beheading may be too much."

"But dunking might not be," Tim said.

"You could put them on the rack," Stacey offered.

"Get upstairs and go to sleep. We'll talk in the morning."

Chapter Seventeen

"**T**hink Fran will send us home?" Luci asked, walking into their room.

Jay started pulling off her clothes. "No. She'll probably just put those little electronic devices on our ankles that beep if you get too far away."

"Like house arrest."

"Yeah."

Luci lay back on her bed. She was so tired she wasn't sure she could undress. "Are you going to take a shower?"

"Yeah. What about you?"

Luci didn't answer. She was asleep.

Daria thumped on the door. "Luci. Jay. It's time for breakfast."

Luci opened her eyes to bright sunlight coming in the window.

"It can't be morning already," Jay groaned.

"It's been this morning for most of my life," Luci said, trying to sit up. "I can't move."

There was another thump at the door. "Are you in there or have you gone exploring again?"

"We're out climbing Mount Olympus. We'll be back for lunch," Jay called.

"Very funny," Daria said grumpily.

They heard her footsteps receding the hallway.

Luci propped up her pillow and managed to sit up in bed. "I never slept in my clothes before."

Jay grinned.

"I feel so grubby."

"Take a quick shower. You don't want to be late for breakfast."

"I'd like to miss it. We're just going to get yelled at."

"Maybe not."

Luci slowly got to her feet and began removing her clothes. "Do you think it was worth it?"

"You bet. Don't you?"

Luci put the dirty clothes in a neat pile on the floor. She'd stick them in a plastic bag after breakfast so when she packed them with her other things, dirt wouldn't get all over everything. "Yes. I guess."

"You didn't tell me last night. What was going on between you and Glin?"

"Nothing."

"Try another answer. That one doesn't work."

Luci twisted her towel. "Don't make more of this than you should. When we got out of the cave, he kissed me. The end."

Jay sat on her bed. "Fantastic!"

"He was being chivalrous."

"Glin likes you."

Luci wrinkled her nose.

"Why do you have such a hard time believing that?"

"Because if I believe it and he doesn't, my heart will fall out and I'll be walking around with a hole in my chest."

Jay went to Luci and hugged her. "You wouldn't, you know. But I don't think you have to worry about it."

"I'm not like you. You're so strong. You can love someone and let it be okay to never see him again."

"Did I ever say it was okay?"

The group was seated around the table, fresh-fruit cups at every place. Luci and Jay rushed into the room and found their places.

Fran looked at them in silence for a long moment, until Luci wanted to dig a hole for herself and crawl in.

"Ladies and gentlemen," Fran began. "I want you to know I called New York this morning to tell them what happened. This was an infraction too serious for me to handle alone. I could make a decision and it might not be suitable."

"Are you sending us home?" Logan asked.

"No."

"Good," Logan replied, and dug into his fruit cup.

Fran put her hand on his arm as he was bringing the spoon to his mouth. "I don't think you understand how dangerous this escapade was."

Logan put the spoon down. "I do. I incorporated all the concerns in the logistics."

Tim groaned and slumped in his chair.

"There should have been no logistics. This was not a military maneuver! You were not on a mission. You are not a member of the SEALS or the Special Forces."

Logan shook his head. "I know that. I took the precautions I thought necessary."

"You're seventeen! You don't know everything that can happen! One of you could have been hurt," Fran said.

"There could have been a cave-in," Tim added.

"What would you have done? You were miles from help. It was dark. This isn't America, where they have rescue choppers waiting on all the foolish people trying stunts they have no business attempting."

"No one got hurt."

"And weren't you lucky that's the case?" Fran said sternly. "How would I explain a serious accident to your father? Think about it, Logan. Maybe you think he'd applaud you for taking this chance, but if anything went wrong, he'd have my head."

Logan nodded. "That's probably true."

"I'm supposed to be taking care of you . . . you . . . brats!"

Glin leaned forward. "Fran, you know me. You know Logan. We are sorry. We know we went beyond the parameters of the tour. We apologize and it won't happen again."

Fran regarded Glin evenly. "This isn't about me getting my feelings hurt, or even that you went out at night. This is about doing something very dangerous. And I don't think you're sorry."

Luci lowered her eyes. Fran was absolutely right. She wasn't sorry. Oh, part of her was. Luci was sorry that she had broken a rule, had betrayed a trust. But she was glad she had gone. The others were right. This was an experience she'd treasure for her entire life. How could she be sorry about that?

There was complete silence at the table.

"The decision from New York is that if you can't agree to abide by all the rules, you cannot be a part of Getaway Tours. I'm not a baby-sitter. None of the guides are. I can't stay up all night long trying to keep track of you. We need to be able to trust you."

"I think we understand that," Glin said.

"So what's the final word. Is this ever going to happen again?"

"If you tell my parents, I probably won't have to worry about it happening again," Luci admitted. "I'll be grounded. Permanently."

"It won't happen again," Glin said.

"No."

Jay shook her head.

Logan picked up his spoon. "Am I going to be held to the strict letter on this promise?"

"Yes!" Fran exclaimed.

"I won't go into any caves at night," Logan promised.

Fran glared at him. "You're incorrigible."

Logan grinned at her.

Fran held her hands over her face for a moment. "Guys."

Tim sat up. "What Fran is trying to say is that we were young once—"

"Tim!"

"Fran still is!" Tim added quickly.

Everyone at the table laughed.

Fran sighed. "I work for Getaway because I'm an adventurer. I've taken chances. I tried to cross the Alps with a donkey in January."

"Another pilgrim route," Tim interjected.

"I'm here to tell you I didn't make it. It can be a dangerous world. You're not in your living room anymore. I want you to explore. I want you to test yourselves. But I don't want you to get hurt, either. And I know because nothing bad happened last night, you don't feel like you made a mistake. You probably feel good about it. You found that thing . . . whatever it is. You went on a treasure hunt. How many people get to do that? It's exciting. And it's something you're going to remember fondly for the rest of your lives. Am I right?"

Luci nodded.

"Yes," Jay replied.

"But you're not adults and I'm responsible for you. I'm here to guide you. Do you understand that? Not just to drag your fannies around France. I'm here to give you some direction."

"I'm sorry," Logan said.

Luci looked at him in surprise. She never thought she'd hear that from him.

Fran leaned over and kissed his cheek. She was about to say something but stopped. Luci thought Fran might have been on the verge of tears.

"Let's eat and get out of this town," Tim suggested.

Everyone began digging into their food.

"Do we have time to see Georges before we leave?" Logan asked.

"Yes," Fran said. "And bring that darn thing back to him."

"Yes, ma'am," Logan replied.

Stacey was on the terrace when Jay and Luci arrived. "Nice play, Shakespeare."

Luci was too tired to wonder what Stacey was getting at, so she just went to her bicycle.

"If you have something to say, say it," Jay told her.

"You managed to spend the night with the guys. Alone. No adults around."

"That's right, we did. So?"

"I find it interesting."

Luci looked up. "Why?"

"You've been like the Four Musketeers from the beginning. You two have monopolized Logan. And Glin."

Luci closed her eyes. "Stacey, you could have come along."

"No one asked me."

"Maybe it was because you didn't seem to want to be part of it. It was all about dead people to you," Jay said. "Pardon us if we didn't guess you'd want to be involved in a treasure hunt."

"I wouldn't!"

"See?"

Jay was missing the obvious this morning. Stacey was jealous. She had been attracted to Logan from the first day and he didn't realize she was alive.

"Stacey, we didn't do this on purpose," Luci said.

"Oh. It was an accident."

"It wasn't that either," Jay replied. "People hang around with people who have the same interests. You have been hanging around with Daria because you both like to shop. I don't have the money to shop. I don't think Luci does, either. We're here to see France. And we tried to see as much of it as we could. As it turns out, Glin and Logan wanted to see France, too."

"Why would I come on the tour if I didn't want to see France?" Stacey asked.

"Maybe you just wanted to see a different part of it," Luci replied.

Logan and Glin left the hotel and walked across the terrace.

Luci looked up and leaned her bike toward Stacey. "Stacey, would you like to go with them? I'm really tired. I don't need to ride this bicycle an inch farther. You take mine and I'll stay here."

Glin stared at Luci.

Logan froze on the steps to the driveway.

"Well . . ." Stacey began.

"Stacey," Daria called from the upstairs window. "Will you come help me pack? I can't get all the stuff into my suitcase."

Logan walked down the rest of the steps.

"Next time," Stacey said. "But thank you for asking." She walked back into the hotel.

"Why would you ask her to go with us?" Jay asked.

"You're the one who found the bee," Glin said. "You have to bring it back to Georges."

"I felt sorry for her."

"That's a wasted emotion," Logan said as he gracefully pushed off on the bicycle.

"I need some coffee," Jay said.

The *serveur* left four café au laits on the table in front of them. They all sipped the coffee. Jay cut the freshly baked croissants into pieces and took one. Luci took another and savored the warm, buttery roll.

"The four of us make a good team," Logan said. "Do you think you'll be taking another tour?"

Jay put down her cup. "This was a gift from a friend. She's been very generous so far, but I don't know if she'll offer to send me on another trip."

"What about you, Luci?"

"I want to travel, but money is a problem."

Logan and Glin nodded.

"How do you do it?" she asked, curious and not a little envious as well.

Glin wiped his hands on a napkin. "I sometimes join my father's band and earn money. It's a trio, and once in a while they need a replacement. Or there'll be a gig where it can be a foursome. Or like Stacey was teasing me, I can perform at fairs. I juggle."

"Really?" Luci asked.

"Uh-huh. My persona is a court jester."

Luci tried to imagine Glin wearing a multicolored costume, juggling knives or apples. "How long have you been doing that?"

"For most of my life. My mother put herself through graduate school by working Renaissance fairs. Sometimes she performed as a belly dancer."

"Now you're kidding me."

"She's very beautiful. It's a traditional form of folk dancing. It's not like what you see in the bad part of town, no clothes and—"

"Of course," Luci replied quickly.

"She doesn't do that anymore."

"I'm sure she doesn't."

"Except on special occasions, to illustrate certain scholarly points."

Luci longed to meet his mother. She must be so cool. The McKennitts were unspeakably plain compared with the Woods family.

In three days, she'd probably never see Glin again. Luci's stomach clenched. Was the coffee too strong? Or was it something else?

"What about you, Logan?" Jay asked. "Where do you live?"

"Atlanta, right now. My grandparents are in Montana. My father flies corporate jets, so he's always going around. We've lived six different places since I started high school. There was Philadelphia, Dallas, Denver, Scottsdale . . . and now Atlanta. It's the perfect job for him. Better than working for an airline where he'd have a schedule. The pay is good and our expenses are fairly low. I think my father would like his own company though. Buy a Learjet and rent it out."

"Jets must be expensive."

Logan nodded. "Maybe one of these days he'll get lucky."

"What'd you say? Positive thinking," Luci said. "I will win the lottery. I will win the lottery."

"I will win the lottery," Logan repeated.

"I will win the lottery," Jay repeated.

"I'm the one who's gonna win the lottery," Glin stated.

"So if one of us does win, do we split the money?" Jay asked.

"Of course," Luci replied.

"Good." Glin smiled. "It's nice to know I'll be taken care of in my old age."

"You know, we only promised not to go in caves at night again."

"Logan . . ." Jay groaned.

"So if it looks like we can afford to go on another tour, we should all go on the same one."

"I won't argue with that," Glin said.

Maybe Luci could get a job and earn the money. Of course, with all her schoolwork, that would be difficult, and her parents had never wanted her to work, since they believed her education was the only priority she should have at this time. Maybe her mother would let her help with the catering business, sautéing those special croutons.

Come on, croutons!

What kind of life did Luci have if she had to pin all her hopes for the future on the success of stale bread cubes?

Logan glanced at his watch. "We'd better hit the road."

Jay downed the last of her coffee. "Yeah, I don't want another lecture from Fran."

"It wasn't as bad as it could have been," Luci admitted as she stood up.

"Considering where we are and how people have

been tortured for answers right here, we got off light."
Glin smiled.

Luci reached into her pocket for her part of the bill.
The bee was safe where she had put it this morning
when she had changed clothes. Maybe it would go into
a museum. Or maybe it would just go back into
Georges's drawer to wait for the next group of gullible
tourists.

Luci didn't believe that. Georges didn't seem like a
con man or a practical joker.

Maybe this bee had just fallen out of the box or bag
when the entire treasure had been removed. That's
why it was on top of the ground.

"You know, if we ever have the chance to come
back, we could bring a metal detector," Luci suggested, getting on her bike.

"Good idea." Jay sounded impressed. "There might
be another bee hanging around."

"Would we give that one to Georges, too?"

"It *is* his cave," Luci said.

Logan pushed off. "It's not *his* cave."

Luci wondered if that was true.

"There must be rules which apply to treasure
hunting," Jay said.

"Of course. Finders keepers, losers weepers," Logan supplied.

"I don't think that would hold up in a court of law,"
Glin pointed out.

"It does. It's international salvage. If you go to all
the trouble to get treasure, it's yours," Logan insisted.

"Doesn't that only apply to shipwrecks?" Luci
asked.

Glin thought for a moment. "I think Logan's almost right."

"In what way am I wrong?" Logan challenged him.

"What difference does it make this time?" Glin asked.

"None," Jay agreed.

"Next time . . ." Logan began.

"Next time we keep all the treasure to ourselves," Glin assured him.

"Like Midas, we'll be. Hoarding it," Luci teased. "Counting."

"We'll count so much we'll have blisters on our fingers." Jay laughed.

"There will be a next time," Logan insisted.

"Positive thinking," Luci said. "We will win the lottery."

"We will!" Logan repeated.

Chapter Eighteen

"*B*onjour!" Georges welcomed them into the cottage. "*Comment allez-vous?*"

"*Bien, merci,*" Jay replied.

"We're fine," Logan said.

Georges clapped his hands together in delight. "*Bon!*"

Luci sat on a wooden chair and glanced around the room. Even if he had chosen to live simply, wouldn't there be a Picasso on the wall or a Grecian statue on the end table?

Maybe he had devoted his life to searching for the treasure and hadn't found it. Perhaps he had enjoyed his own Grail quest so much that he wanted them to have some fun, too.

Luci rested her hand on her pocket.

None of that explained the gold bee.

Logan settled himself on the sofa. "We went to the cave last night."

"*Ah, oui?*"

"We found it easily," Glin added.

"The map is good."

Luci forced herself to sit still. She wanted to hold out the bee and ask Georges directly where it had come from. She wanted to know if he had ever been in the cave.

"It's a surprise that no one ever found the cave before," Logan said as he placed the map on the table.

Georges shook his head. *"Non.* There are many caves in the area. It is not difficult to find something when you know where to look."

Luci held back a smile. It seemed to her that Logan was trying to play a game with Georges in an attempt to find out how much the old man knew without revealing what they knew. Georges was far too canny to be tricked by a teenager, no matter how smart.

"And you said you had never gone into this cave yourself?" Logan asked.

"I was injured." Georges patted his leg.

Luci thought that was an interesting answer to Logan's direct question. Georges completely avoided responding. When had he been injured? Was it before or after he had found the cave? Did the injury really have anything to do with mountain climbing or had he fallen off his bicycle after having one too many Pernods at the local café?

They weren't going to know.

"Luci," Logan said.

She removed the bee from her pocket.

"Luci found this in an inner chamber," Logan said.

Luci crossed to Georges and held out the bee to him. "Someone said it might be from the Merovingians."

Georges's face lit up as he took the bee. "Isn't it beautiful?"

Luci studied his face. Had he ever seen it before?

She took a step back. Why had she become so distrustful?

"It's lovely," Glin said.

"It must be very old," Jay added.

Luci watched Georges's fingers as he turned the bee over and over in his hands. "What will you do with it?" she asked.

Georges closed his hand around it.

Glin stood. "Shouldn't it be taken to a university or an expert to determine what it is?"

"*Bien sûr*. Yes, of course. We must learn what this is. This is an important find."

"Is it part of the Cathar Treasure?" Logan asked.

"Yes, yes. It might be that."

"Is it the treasure Saunière found?" Jay asked.

"I think it must be," Georges replied. "How excited he must have been when he came upon the treasure. How happy to think what good he could do for his people."

"And your great-aunt," Luci added.

"After his death, Marie lived well for many years."

There was a long pause. Perhaps Georges was remembering his great-aunt. Perhaps he was remembering all his searches. Whatever was going through his mind, these were memories he wasn't going to share.

Glin went to the door. "I think it's about time we got back. We're leaving this morning."

The others followed Glin to the door.

"I hope you had a good time in Les Thermes," Georges said as he opened the door for them. "I hope you will remember us fondly."

"I'm sure we will," Luci replied.

Glin stepped outside. "Thank you."

"*Merci,*" Jay said.

Logan headed to the bicycles.

Luci paused on the doorstep. "Monsieur Denarnaud, we have so many questions which haven't been answered."

"Yes?"

"Did you know what we would find in the cave?"

Glin raised his eyebrows.

"I had hoped you would find something in the cave. One must hope," George stated.

"Did you know what was in the cave?" Luci persisted.

Georges held the bee up to the sunlight. The surface had been scratched severely over the years, but it still glinted. "I suspected. This has been my life."

He studied the bee with the same expression that a young child would look at a Christmas tree. With wonder, delight, and love.

Luci believed him.

"And now it is your life, *aussi.*" Georges paused. "Perhaps this belongs to you. You found it." He held out the bee to Luci.

"No," she started. "It's all yours."

"If there had been two . . ." Georges began.

"Then we'd split fifty-fifty," Luci said.

"As you say. Fifty-fifty." Georges smiled. "*Merci,*" he said. "*Mille mercis.*"

"Thank you," Luci replied.

"*Au revoir,*" Jay said.

"*Au revoir,*" Georges replied, and waved as they got on their bicycles.

"He's lying."

"Logan!" Luci gasped.

"I don't believe any of it," Logan said.

Luci pedaled harder. "I do."

"I'm not sure," Jay admitted. "He sounded very convincing. . . ."

"I agree with Luci," Glin said. "I think everything he said was true."

"That's fine," Logan replied. "He didn't say he'd never been in the cave."

"What difference does it make? We were able to go into a cave and find a treasure. What if he put it there twenty years ago and asks every tourist to find it?"

"And no one has but us?" Luci added.

"It's not our bee anyway," Jay pointed out. "It's his bee."

"But it was our Grail quest," Glin said.

Luci nodded. It was a chance in a lifetime and Georges was right. She would remember Les Thermes fondly. If he had arranged it all, she was grateful he would be so kind.

"That's enough for me," Jay said, echoing Luci's thoughts.

"Is it enough for you, Logan?" Glin asked.

Logan didn't answer immediately.

Luci knew what bothered him. It was not having the loose ends tied up all neat and perfect. He wasn't interested in having the treasure. He was interested in having the answers.

"Maybe if you're not getting the answers you want, you're not asking the right questions," Luci offered.

"New-age mumbo jumbo. You've been talking too much to Aimee," Logan said.

"Not at all. Did you have a good time? Did you find friends? Did you learn more about yourself and the world?"

Glin smiled at Luci.

Logan shrugged. "Okay. So even if the answer to all those questions is yes . . . where's the lost treasure of the Cathars?"

The Getaway van was parked in front of the hotel as they rode the bicycles into the hotel courtyard.

"You're impossible," Jay exclaimed, getting off the bike.

Fran was waiting on the terrace for them. "And you're late. Get upstairs, get your luggage and get back here!"

Luci and Jay met Daria on the stairs. She was struggling with her suitcase and duffel bag. Stacey was following her.

"Don't dawdle," Stacey said. "I want to leave."

"We'll be right there."

"Uh-huh."

Luci opened the door to her room and began throwing clothes into her suitcase. "Do you have a plastic bag?"

Jay tossed a bag across the room.

Luci stuffed her dirty shirt into it.

Jay zipped her bag shut. "It was good, huh?"

"Great."

Luci picked up her jeans and gave them a shake to straighten the legs. Something hit the floor.

"What's that?" Jay reached down.

"Oh. That's the coin Glin threw in the dirt."

Jay picked it up and looked at it curiously. "I don't think so."

"Sure it is."

Jay turned the coin over.

Luci stuffed the jeans in the bag. "I thought it was a quarter, but then it felt like something else. So it must be a franc."

"It's something else, all right."

Luci went over to Jay. It was a roundish metal disk, yellow in color, with some lettering on it.

"What is it? That's not French."

"No, it's Latin. What's it say? Septimus?" Luci could barely make out the inscription.

"Luci . . ."

Luci opened the door to the room to see Aimee walking by. Grabbing her arm, she dragged her into the room.

"Aimee!"

"Luci!" Aimee laughed.

"What is this?"

Jay held out the coin.

"You found more stuff? Cool." Aimee took the coin and studied it. "I'm no authority on antiquities."

"So you think this is old?" Luci asked.

"Very. It's a Roman coin."

"Roman?" Jay repeated.

"Why not? The Visigoths sacked Rome. They

brought their treasure here. Isn't that what you've been looking for?"

Luci and Jay stared at each other, then at the coin.

Aimee gave the coin a flip and it went into the air, turning over and over. Luci held out her hand and the coin dropped into it.

"Better get downstairs," Aimee said, and left the room.

"Roman?" Jay asked.

"Is this the treasure?"

"Is it ours?"

"Girls!" Fran shouted from downstairs. "Hurry up!"

Luci stuffed the coin into her pocket and threw the rest of her things into her bag. "Do we have everything? I feel like I'm going to leave something!"

Jay ran around the room, turning over the bedspreads, looking on all flat surfaces. "We've got everything."

"Are you positive?"

"Be serious. We didn't have anything to begin with."

"I guess." Luci closed the suitcase and patted her pocket. The coin was still there.

"Need some help?" Glin asked at the doorway.

"Sure. That would be great."

Glin picked up Luci's suitcase and they all went downstairs.

"Mademoiselle Hamilton! Mademoiselle Hamilton!" The concierge ran after them as they left the hotel.

Jay paused and he handed her a note.

Glin helped Luci with her luggage and then they got inside the van. Jay sat down next to her.

"What did the concierge want?" Luci asked.

Jay opened the note. "Sam called from Norway."

"Oops," Luci said. "Did he leave a number?"

"No." Jay refolded the note. "He'll call again."

"Are you sure?"

"Uh-huh." Jay smiled.

Fran got in the van and closed the door. "All present and accounted for?"

"Yes, now can we please *leave*?" Stacey asked.

Tim started the engine and the van began to pull away from the hotel. The village of Les Thermes passed by the windows.

Luci touched her pocket. She could feel the coin. This was going to be a major surprise to the guys, but she wasn't going to tell them just yet. Luci was going to wait a bit.

She turned to Glin and smiled. "Tell me, Glin. What would be served at a Grail feast?"